ADAM E

THE

MIDNIGHT

WAR

Paperback: 978-1-80227-123-2
eBook: 978-1-80227-124-9

DEDICATION

To my family, without whom this wouldn't be possible.
To Laura, who made me put the peonies in.
To my little one; meet you soon.

ABOUT THE AUTHOR

Adam Elliott was raised in a small village in Berkshire. Fascinated with Science Fiction from a very young age, he spent his youth either reading through the entire Star Wars novel collection or blasting aliens on Halo. He spends a lot of his time with his wife and Collie-cross dog, who, he later discovered, was crossed with a Jack Russell and somehow inherited the challenging traits of both breeds. This is his first book to be published and he is over the moon that it will be arriving around the same time as his first child.

PROLOGUE

The latest impact was the one that crippled the cruiser. It was the one that the crew had been hoping wouldn't come – the one that meant they would never see their loved ones again. *A routine mission,* they had told him, *reports of pirates along the trade route.* What a load of shit. Three months going backwards and forwards along the trade route, nothing happening but dull repetition, nought to show for it and now this? *I should have taken the offer of retirement,* James thought to himself. He knew they didn't stand a chance. As Captain of the *H.M.S. Adroit,* he had always carried the responsibility of caring for his crew well upon his shoulders. They'd been in a few tight spots before but this battle was unwinnable and James knew it. He hoped that he had managed to keep that knowledge off his face but doubted it.

"Flight, get me a way out of here!" James burned with the desire to do something, anything in the vain hope of escape. A second later, even that hope had died.

"I'm sorry, sir. We can't calculate a way to get to hyperspace. The gravity wells keep shifting quicker than we can keep up." Those words, spoken softly but clearly, were the death knell of everyone on the ship.

"Sound the evacuation," James ordered quietly. "Get as many people off this ship as you can and pray to his Majesty that someone picks up our distress signal."

"Captain," the Tactical Officer, Ensign Forde signalled for his attention. "They've stopped firing."

Everyone turned to the display screen at the front of the bridge. All vibrations stopped, the echoes of the blasts slowly fading away into nothing. Something was moving but even the beadiest eyes wouldn't have been able to make out any details. The ships (if they were even that) were black – the sort of black that absorbed all light. Nothing could be seen of them but the outlines where they blocked out the stars behind.

We never saw them coming. What do they want? No sooner was their collective attention focused on the screen, than there was a click and the *H.M.S. Adroit* lost all power. *Now what?*

Unable to see, James could nevertheless pick up on the sudden intake of breath that came from Ensign Forde.

"Captain, we picked up movement on the scanners just before we lost power. Looked like those things were breaking down." His voice caught as if about to break and he fell into silence. The emergency lighting on the bridge kicked in, providing a dim illumination.

"Breaking down how?"

"Like they'd split into a hundred smaller ships." Ensign Forde looked confused, his face highlighted in a deep red. "What in the worlds could that mean, sir?"

Swiftly sifting through all the possibilities, only one stood out as likely. "A boarding action." James had thought it couldn't get any worse than before, but if this was what he thought it was…

We have to move quickly. If they're planning to board, they want something from us. James stood from his command chair, moving to the arms locker at the door to the bridge. He keyed in the code to unlock it, took out a pistol and threw it to one of his officers before taking one himself. He slid the magazine out of the bottom to check that it was fully loaded then pushed it back into place before turning to face the surviving members of his bridge crew. His suspicions were confirmed as multiple impacts sounded across the hull.

"This is what we're gonna do." James faced his crew with a heavy heart, giving them the speech he had hoped never to have to give. "They're coming for us. We don't know who they are or what they want but I do know something. We must not allow them to access our systems, as they'll then know everything about us: Who we are, where we come from, our weapons capabilities; even our troop numbers and ship counts."

As he spoke, he looked each member of his crew in the eyes in turn. Some began to weep, understanding what the next words out of his mouth were going to be.

"Forde, wipe the system and set the self-destruct. If I remember my specs correctly, that should take about seven minutes, yes?"

"Yes, sir."

"Good lad. Set it now. For the rest of us, our job is to stop whatever comes through that door long enough for the system to wipe itself. Think now – it's not just our lives that are at an end; it could be the life of everyone in the Empire if we don't pull this next bit off. Understood?"

A chorus of "yes, sirs" rang out as his crew spread out and took cover around the room. Buoyed by their bravery, James took his own position behind his console and aimed his weapon at the main entrance, his hand shaking violently with the fear that he had managed to keep off of his face. He nodded at his Flight Officer, Ensign Desoto, who slapped the panel next to the door, using the remaining power to seal the bulkhead against the outside threat.

"Ladies and gentlemen, it's been an honour to serve with you."

Now completely focused on the door ahead, the room went quiet. A minute crept by, then two. A sudden scream made James jump. He looked around both for the source of the noise and to check that his skittishness hadn't been noticed by his crew. After a few seconds, he decided that the noise was coming from beyond the door. Another minute went by with more screams being added to the cacophony of death. Then, again, silence.

They're here. A drop of sweat coming down his forehead ran into his eye and James moved to mop it up. As he did so, there was a movement to his right. Turning, James fired his pistol at the black murk that had risen from one of the vents. There was another scream, definitely human and James had but a second to recognise Desoto, now bleeding from a gunshot wound to his right shoulder before the blackness hit him and he lost consciousness.

#

James came round quickly. Shaking his head, he tried to see what was happening around him. Slowly, ever so slowly, it came into focus. He could see nothing but the bodies of his crew, all of whom had been killed by pistol rounds. The sight of Ensign Forde's face stretched into a permanent scream would be burned into his memory for the rest of his life.

Did we do this to each other? He thought in despair. His eyes settled on the countdown timer on the display screen. It had stopped with three seconds left to go. The numbers blinked at him mutely as he stared at it in horror.

A shadow sprung from the darkness around the periphery of the bridge. Without warning, James found himself hanging limply in the air, unable to move, to do anything other than breathe and look forward.

What new devilry is this? We don't have any Mages on the ship, how is this happening?

His body started moving towards the main console like a puppet on a string, every movement out of his control. He found himself putting in his command codes, opening the database for anyone to go through. That having been done, he found himself floating above the ground once again. He lost these moments between the flashes of conscious thought as if jumping forward through time.

Like a movie, he started to see his memories playing before his very eyes, slowly at first but then quickening as he got closer to his adult life, his years in the military.

They're controlling this; they're using me to find what they want. In his mind, the memories settled on one particular day - a day of triumph for the Empire. It was the day that it had been announced that they were to take part in the Dùbhlan, the annual combat competition between two randomly selected races in the Hegemony.

For the Empire to take part was unheard of, especially as they kept themselves from the rest. It meant that they were finally being accepted as equals in the political landscape of the Milky Way – it meant everything to Earth's military.

He remembered that day perfectly – remembered the news channels showing the announcement over and over. The same footage playing on a loop with countless holo personalities debating what this would mean for the Empire. The most regularly played clip was of officials on a podium stepping up to accept the challenge on behalf of the King.

There was something that his attention was drawn to then; something that he hadn't really noticed at the time. Behind the podium stood a band of Mages, the special ones from each race that could use Magick. Each of them would have been taken at a young age, then raised to manipulate space and time with nothing but a thought.

His mind moved to another image, this one a report of a missing girl being broadcast over the news networks. The young girl was of fair complexion and the photo they were using had clearly been taken when this girl was happy, before she had been abducted from her home. James hadn't paid attention to this report at the time but somehow it had remained in his mind.

Feeling rushed back into his body. Despite all of his best efforts, he hadn't been able to stop these people, whoever they were, from finding the information they sought. Pressure began to mount on his skin, not in one patch but everywhere, getting increasingly painful by the second.

The black shadow drifted towards the door. Strangely, he felt something like satisfaction emanating from the thing. Unable to even think any longer, James's last moments became nothing but pain as he opened his mouth in a wordless scream.

1

CHAPTER ONE

It moved. It Kingdamned floated! All by itself – this time she hadn't moved a muscle. Well, that wasn't strictly true. Danica Shaw (or Danny to her friends, if only she had any) had moved it with the power of her mind. Magick! She hadn't believed them when they'd told her that she had tested positive for the ability to control Magick. Such a small, innocuous thing, a pen, yet it had the potential to change her life beyond all recognition. She opened her eyes and saw exactly what she expected to – a plain little ballpoint pen, hovering in her line of sight about six feet away from her face.

"I never thought you could do it," came a voice from behind her; "an irrelevance like you with the sort of power the Royal Family could only dream of having. Imagine my surprise at being proven wrong."

Danny's head snapped round and she saw a tall man standing in the doorway to her cabin. She'd only seen him once before when he had arrived unexpectedly at the front door of her family's small home. She hadn't known who he was but her parents certainly had – as soon as they saw him standing there, garbed only in a black robe with a squad of Royal Marines behind him, they tried slamming the door in his face. She could still hear her mum screaming at her to run, not to look back as the door shattered and sent debris flying into the hallway…

#

Run she had; out the back door and into the alleyway behind their house, around the corner into a second smaller footpath, surrounded on both sides by tall apartment buildings. So many people living so close together – she screamed as she ran, desperate for anyone around her to notice that something was wrong. She heard only the echoes of her voice bouncing back at her, the voices overlapping and forming a broken choir begging for help.

She kept going even after she heard the gunfire coming from behind her and the whistle of bullets zinging past her head. She was young but she knew what that noise meant. It was a common noise in the cities of Earth, signalling the end of another life and the start of another mother's pain with each burst of sound. Squinting through the tears running down her face that threatened to make her almost blind, she'd tried to dart out onto the main road but had come to a jarring halt only metres from her target.

Unable to move, she had cried and grieved for her parents until the very man who was now standing in front of her appeared in her vision, having sauntered around the corner. With no hesitation, he had slapped her. She stopped crying, shocked that this man, this random person who had no right to be doing this, would dare touch her.

"So, you have spirit," the man had said, "yet it remains to be seen if you have anything else of use to me." He tilted his head slightly, a slow smile spreading across his sickly pale face. "Come, no more of this useless struggle."

Danny fell to the ground, control of her limbs returning swiftly. Like a shot, she was back up and running, desperately hoping that if she could just make it around the next corner, she could escape and… blackness took her.

#

"It will not be long before you lose your memories of your previous life; even of your parents", the man said. "You look like an insignificant nothing and you are, but the power within you, the raw potential... Oh, what we are going to do with you."

Danny shuddered without really knowing why, understanding only that this man now had control over whether she lived or died. She lowered her head as if reflecting on his words when really, she was trying to get a better look at his face through the long, blonde locks of hair cascading from her scalp.

He was tall and thin like a whip but the way he held himself told Danny that this man was used to being obeyed. He was wearing the black robe again (she hadn't seen him wear anything else) with nothing to cover his bare, bulbous head. Overall, he looked rather plain. His eyes were his one outstanding quality – a verdant green, they almost seemed to be glowing with an inner power. As Danny thought this to herself, the man again smiled.

"Plain I may look but you would do well to pay attention to me when I am talking. From this point on, child, I am your lord and master. If you perform well, I will give you power and rewards, more than you have ever imagined in your ridiculous existence." His next words turned Danny's stomach. "If you displease me or if you fail at any of the tasks set for you, I will ensure that the rest of your life is spent in agony, without even a ray of hope to light up the darkness. I will, in short, destroy you."

The threat didn't sit well with Danny. She felt a surge of anger and directed it at this man. *Kill him. Destroy the smug look on his face and run away.* She focused on his neck, visualising what she wanted, almost hearing the snap of bone as it shifted and dropped him to the deck. Since she had been a child, she had found that she could make things happen just by wishing them into existence. She hoped that this was another one of those times.

Nothing happened. The man smiled again, a genuine look of amusement showing on his face. "You should know by now, that will not work." Danny again lost control of her body, this time feeling herself flying through the air before coming to a bone-jarring stop against the wall. "Shall we stop playing games? Would you like to know why you are really here?"

Danny nodded meekly, her vision blurred from the impact. It returned swiftly, allowing her to focus once more on the man. She dropped to the floor but her reflexes were sharp enough to brace herself. Landing on her feet, she turned to the man, asking, "What do you want from me?"

"Ah, my dear – it is not I who wants something from you. Instead, you should be asking yourself, what can you give me?" The man turned to the door as if to leave then spun on his heels. "Come with me, now!" Danny followed the command without hesitation, not willing to test the limits of this stranger's patience any further.

#

As she stepped through the door, she realised straight away that she wasn't on Earth anymore. She was in a long, cold and brightly illuminated metal corridor that stretched off far into the distance. It wasn't so much the look of where she was as the feeling that gave it away. Now that she was moving, she realised that she felt heavier than normal, though not by much. She was on a spaceship! She had seen enough movies to realise that she was on a warship, knowing without really understanding that the military set the gravity slightly higher to encourage denser muscle growth in their soldiers.

The man turned to his right and started walking briskly, forcing Danny to have to jog to keep up. They walked like this for two hundred metres (Danny was counting her steps as she went) then stopped in front of another unmarked portal. They had yet to come across another person on the short journey and Danny wondered where everyone was.

"Now, before this goes any further, I have some simple instructions for you to follow. Are you listening?" Danny nodded. "Good. You will refer to me as the Lord Regent, or sir when I am addressing you. Do you understand?"

"Yes, sir." The two simple words caused another sickly smile to break out across the man's face at the small victory. Danny felt her face flush in shame at how easily she had conformed to his expectations.

"Good girl. I am about to show you your future; not using Magick, but instead, using something more mundane. There will be people beyond this door who do not know who you are. Your identity has, for the moment, been deemed a secret – do not attempt to speak to anyone. I will know if you are thinking about it and the punishment will be severe."

Danny finally understood that this man – this "Lord Regent" – would genuinely hurt her if she disobeyed. With this understanding came hope. Now that she knew what to expect from him, she could buy herself some time and with time would come a means of escape.

"It's amazing what small minds will cling to when all else seems lost," the Lord Regent wasn't happy. Without another word, he pressed the door's opening mechanism and the hatch slid back into its recess without any noise. The room beyond came into view and Danny gasped.

She was looking at a vibrantly coloured planet, greener and larger than Earth. She could see clear continents framed by an azure blue ocean, with brilliantly white clouds dancing in the upper atmosphere. She had never seen anything so beautiful and was saddened when she realised that she hadn't had the chance to see Earth from orbit on the outward journey.

She turned her attention to the room that the Lord Regent had brought her to. She had to strain her neck back to see the ceiling and it took her two heartbeats to notice that the room was full of uniformed people. There was a stage set up against the great, reinforced glass wall that stretched from bulkhead to bulkhead with a lectern facing away from the marvel behind and towards the assembled men and women. A huge banner displaying the coat of arms of the Royal Family was flying behind the lectern and many people in the crowd were waving small flags in excitement.

The Lord Regent led Danny through the crowd so far that she lost her bearings, unable to tell exactly which direction they had come from. She had never been in such a densely packed room before. They stopped close to the front and he bent down and whispered in her ear. "This, child, is your new home." Another shiver went down her back when he touched it, causing her to move instinctively away from him.

Danny gasped. She had never been off Earth before and the planet spread out in front of her filled her mind with wonder. It was so unlike her home planet which had been all but destroyed by warfare when the British Empire took control. The country where she lived was still experiencing problems from radioactive fallout from the nuclear bombs that had been used by the Royals to cement their control. Greenery was rare and to see it in such abundance was incredible.

The noise in the room began to subside as an older man stepped up to the podium. Wearing a full dress uniform with rows upon rows of medals pinned to his chest, this man looked like a warrior. Danny thought he looked sad and wondered what this man had seen in his lifetime.

"Ladies and Gentlemen. Today is a proud day for the Empire. After decades of near conflict with the Hegemony, we have finally begun to be seen as equals on the galactic stage. Our actions in the coming weeks will show that we are not only able to shoulder the burden – but that we are entitled to!" The crowd roared its appreciation, waving their flags and cheering louder and louder until the man at the front motioned for quiet. "I have faith and confidence that you will represent the British Empire to the best of your abilities and do so in such a way that we will never be looked down on again. Ladies and Gentleman, welcome to Midway!"

2

CHAPTER TWO

His coffee was cold and woe betide the aide that didn't get him a fresh mug. General Ariel Webb sat back in his comfortable leather chair and began rubbing his eyes. On his desk were numerous datapads and his computer was pinging constantly with messages to read, forms to sign and fates to decide. *What I wouldn't give for someone else to be doing this,* he thought and spent a minute in the happy place he kept specifically for moments like this, then realised that this self-pitying behaviour wouldn't get any work done.

He forced himself to sit to attention once more and began to read through one of the numerous reports on the state of the 1st Royal Earth Division. Full readiness across the board and morale had never been higher - not that difficult considering this division had been thrown together three months ago when it was announced they would be taking part in the Dùbhlan. Twelve thousand soldiers put in a mixing pot with no bonds between them other than pride at representing the Royal Family. Ariel had been given five divisions along with a few small units of Special Forces. Sixty thousand men and women – all willing and able to die for a family that didn't care one scrap about them. The finest men and women he had ever served with, he was sure. Now, they only had to prove it.

"Sir?" A knock at the door signalled the best thing to happen to him so far this morning. "Coffee for you, sir, along with a couple of custard creams."

"Thank you, Davies. Custard creams; what a treat. Leave them on the desk, would you?"

"Of course, sir." Davies placed the mug carefully on the desk, swept up the old one and glanced at his commanding officer. He thought that the General looked tired which was understandable considering he had been pulling all-nighters to get everything prepared for this most glorious moment in the history of the Empire. "Is there anything else I can do for you, sir?"

"No thank you, Davies," Ariel replied, "unless you can take over the paperwork for me...?" He enjoyed the look of panic that swept across Davies' face. "On second thought, why don't you go and find Colonel Brydges and ask him to come and join me? I'm sure I can handle this in the meantime. Take a custard cream with you."

The look of relief on Davies' face was palpable. "Yes, sir, right away." He almost ran out of the office, ignoring the offer of a biscuit.

Ariel chuckled to himself. *At least I can still put the fear of the King into them,* he thought, bemused. He settled back into his chair and began the battle against the insane make-work that he had somehow found himself stuck with. When he had signed up for service all those years ago, he had thought that he would be helping people, not destined to become a desk jockey. He felt a blossom of pain shoot up the side of his back, a timely reminder, along with the grey hairs sprouting in his hair and moustache, that he had done the running around years ago. It was time for someone else to do it.

#

Another, louder knock at the door startled Ariel who had been so absorbed in his work that he hadn't heard the doorbell chime for attention. A quick look down at his uniform confirmed that he was still looking smart before he pressed the intercom into the waiting room.

"Come."

The hatch opened and Colonel Brydges entered the room, looking for all the world like the perfect soldier. Six foot six inches tall and built like a brick shithouse, his uniform was immaculate as was the inch-perfect salute he offered the General when he came to a halt.

"Colonel Brydges. Reporting as ordered, sir."

Returning the salute, Ariel pointed to the only other chair in the room. "Have a seat, John. No need to be so formal." John took the seat that was offered and sat quietly, adjusting his uniform until it was regulation ready again and waiting for Ariel to announce why he had been summoned from his final preparations.

He snuck a look around and the room and thought it was rather spartan, the only real consideration to comfort being the chair that the General was sat in. He wondered how much it had cost to import the chair from where he guessed it originated – Earth.

"The Hegemony have announced who we'll be facing in the Dùbhlan, John. Care to hazard a guess?"

John shook his head. There were too many possibilities for him to guess and he didn't want to look ignorant in front of the General. "Respectfully, sir, it could be any of them. It's meant to be completely random, isn't it?" The look that went across Ariel's face made his stomach turn. That meant bad news.

"It's supposed to be random but with the opposition we've been given… I have a feeling there's nothing the Hegemony would like to see more than us losing this contest. They've paired us up with the Lukratza," Ariel announced glumly. "They've paired us up with the only species in the Hegemony bred specifically for war."

John felt his heart sink and he scrambled to remember as much about the announced opposition as he could. It took him only a few seconds for the memories to come back, the time spent with the intelligence officers before they embarked from Earth clearly being a good decision.

The Lukratza were a reptilian race from a planet coreward from Earth, the exact location of which was currently unknown. For centuries, they had been the largest part of the Hegemony's military arm, providing more ships and troops than any number of the other races combined. Their military prowess and ruthlessness were legendary – the best example was when they had been sent to a planet to counter a rebellion launched by the native species. There were no survivors. The Hegemony had expunged the species' name from the record and anyone found to be using it was executed without a trial.

"Well, shit. We'll have to be at our best just to keep them at bay, let alone have a shot at beating them," John mused. He wondered how the galaxy knew about the suppressed rebellion if there were no survivors.

"You are correct. As you know, you're going to be the operational commander for the contest. I want you to work up a plan and get it to me by the end of tomorrow," Ariel ordered. "It needs to be a good one. Before you go, talk me through the rules of engagement one last time. I'm getting old, you see, and need reminding of these things." The struggle of keeping a straight face nearly got the better of him and he feigned a cough, moving his hand to cover his mouth on the off chance that John had noticed.

John doubted that the General was getting old and suspected that this was just a ploy to test him again. The General was clearly upset about not being directly in control of his forces and was looking for reassurance that he had handed them over to the right person. John would give it to him.

He took a second to straighten one of the medals on his chest that he had noticed was slightly out of position, using the time to quickly check he had all the information he needed in his head. Once done, he settled back into his chair and looked directly at the General.

"Yes, sir. The Dùbhlan is an interspecies contest held every year between two random species from the Hegemony. This is the first time that we know of in recorded history that a civilisation from outside the Hegemony has been invited to compete. If there are two societies in dispute, they can request to have the matter settled in this contest as open warfare is prohibited by the Hegemony," John paused and waited for the

General to confirm that he was correct so far. The General nodded once at him and he ploughed on.

"Each of the competing species can field up to fifty thousand troops with up to ten thousand held in reserve. Technology levels are determined by the lesser-developed species of the two as decided by the ruling Hegemon. The contest is overseen by the order of Mages who have a stronghold called the Citadel in close proximity but off to the south of the battlefield. They are the only ones allowed a permanent presence on Midway and have the final say over who wins. They are also solely responsible for censuring any contestants found to be in breach of the rules. The contest can be decided in one of two ways – total obliteration or by concession." He tilted his head as he checked that he had presented all of the information he knew of. "Have I missed anything, sir?"

Ariel looked pensive as he processed John's words. He began staring off into space, lost in the recesses of his mind as he evaluated the information, trying to see it from a fresh perspective. Eventually, he looked across to the Colonel and nodded. "You are. Just remember, there are more ways than just those two that could lead to a loss. Do not allow the death of every soldier under your command to be the one that breaks us. I want you to bring as many people back alive from this barbaric practice as you can."

"I'll do my best, sir."

"I believe you, John. You're one of the most competent people I've ever met and I chose you specifically because of your reputation. Now's your opportunity to stake your claim as my replacement when I go - which could be any day now."

John smiled at the General again, sensing the humour and responding in kind. "I doubt that, sir. You look fit as a fiddle."

"Get out, you ruffian."

John stood from the chair, saluted the General once more and helped himself to a biscuit from the table after Webb pointed at them.

"These are good, sir. Are these genuine custard creams?"

3

CHAPTER THREE

The gargantuan hangar of the H.M.S *Excellence* was in a state of absolute pandemonium. After three weeks of waiting in orbit over Midway, the order had finally come to deploy the waiting forces into the almost legendary jungles below. Technicians carted heavy boxes of ordnance into the back of waiting dropships, pilots made final checks on their birds and soldiers mustered in their units. Knowing their jobs intimately, the appearance of chaos was only that. Each of them knew what was coming – death and glory – but not one of them were worried, instead, making light of the situation as soldiers were often known to do.

"Gonna kick some lizard ass!" shouted Private Baker, slamming his right fist against his chest. The noise from the metals smacking together made him jump despite knowing that it would be coming and he grinned sheepishly at his Sergeant. "Right, Sarge?"

Sergeant Geoff Reynolds smiled to himself. Baker was a new recruit to the squad and was still settling in but the kid had stones, standing up for himself when the rest of his squad were trying to test him. Give him enough time and he would shape up to be as good as the rest of them, possibly even better than Reynolds himself – the kid had potential as well as a spine.

"Correct, Baker. We're gonna make them sorry they ever thought about challenging the Empire." *Let's have some fun*, Reynolds thought to himself. "But, son, have you ever seen a Lukratza in the flesh?"

Baker shook his head. "Not in the flesh, Sarge, but I've run the simulations just like everyone else."

"Oh, good. You've run the simulations. That means you know they're almost nine feet tall with scales as thick as battleship armour and teeth that could tear right through a tank?"

"Mmm… yes, sir?"

"And you'll also know that they can blend into the jungle so well that you'll never see them coming and they're faster than a horse at full gallop?"

Despite his bravado a few moments earlier, Baker now looked decidedly pale. "I guess," he stuttered, only to be rescued by Corporal Johnson.

"Don't listen to him, rookie, he's only playing with you." Johnson burst out laughing, "By the King, you should see the look on your face! You'd think that you'd seen a ghost!"

The rest of the squad joined in with the raucous laughter and after a few seconds of trying unsuccessfully to keep a stern face, Reynolds did too. "All right, kids, time to fall in." His squad moved into position, a single line of Special Forces troops standing to attention in front of him. They were immaculately turned out, not only proud of themselves but wanting to show the Sergeant that they respected him.

"This, boys and girls, is the real thing. Our orders are to land ahead of the main force and establish a beachhead here, in this valley," he gestured towards a holographic display that had materialised behind him when he started his briefing. "This position is where HQ are gonna be based and we're going in to make sure the Lukratza haven't prepared any surprises for Colonel Brydges and his team. I want this to go by the book. Once we touch down, I want the four of you out the door ASAP," he pointed at Johnson and Baker, as well as Privates Haley and Sinclair. "Two left and two right. Sweep the initial areas, report any contact then move a hundred yards out and set a perimeter. If you make contact, light them up. Got it?"

"Sir, yes sir!" The squad's reply was deafening – they were up for this. As some of the most highly trained soldiers in the royal army, this was what they had spent their entire careers preparing for. They were ready – and they were eager.

"Move out!" Reynolds ordered his squad and then watched them file into the waiting dropship, loaded for bear. He swung his Bergen over his shoulder, checked his rifle was secure and followed them into the unknown.

#

Surrounded by a vast fleet of warships, the battleship H.M.S. *Excellence* looked as insignificant as an ant in a stream of workers when viewed from afar. In reality, the *Excellence* was over two kilometres long, bristling with grapeshot, missile pods and laser cannons, interspersed here and there by the gaping maws of docking bays. Like all British ships, the battleship was angular in design with a rounded, almost pointed bow, a throwback to the days when ships sailed across the vast oceans of Earth rather than the open nothingness of space.

Although monstrous in size, when compared to the other human ships lazily making their way around Midway, the H.M.S. *Excellence* was not the largest ship in the fleet. It would have been dwarfed by the much bigger *Supreme*-class carriers back in the Sol System but the Dùbhlan was meant to be a land-based conflict – and so the carriers had been left in dock, still awaiting their moment of glory.

A lone dropship disembarked the *Excellence* and spun on its axis, aiming down to Midway below. A sudden flash announced that it had fired its thruster and it began sailing towards its target. For a while, it was the only object visibly moving in the immediate area, yet that didn't last; without any fanfare, hundreds of dropships fell out of the waiting human ships and began their descent, like a swarm of locusts moving on to a new area after devastating the last. The light from each thruster ignition highlighted the fleet mustered in orbit looking for all the worlds like a

New Year's firework display. There was no sound to be heard but the movement and light show both announced the same thing – the royal forces were here, and they were here to stay.

#

An hour later, there was no trace remaining of the dropships or the troops securely held inside them. The fleet continued to move along the path that had been set for it. On the bridge of the *Excellence*, General Webb turned a quizzical eye to his fleet counterpart, Admiral Leystrom.

"Not long now until we get started properly. Colonel Brydges is still aboard but will be departing as soon as Sergeant Reynold's squad sounds the all-clear. Once that happens, I get to put my feet up and twiddle my thumbs until the casualty reports start coming in. What about you, George, what's on your to-do list?"

Leystrom turned from the real-time holographic representation of the battlefield spread out in the middle of the room and faced Webb. "Me, Ariel? Similar. The only thing I have to do is wait until your grunts, however many of them survive, need a lift back to Earth. I hear that any survivors can expect a triumphant return and their choice of posting anywhere in the Empire."

It was true – the King had announced that should they win, any survivors would be honoured beyond their wildest dreams. It was said that the King himself would meet the men and women who remained and it was well known that anything the King touched turned to gold, metaphorically speaking. The flip-side, of course, was that if they lost the Dùbhlan (and there was a high chance of that), dishonour and potentially even execution waited for the disgraced soldiers.

"You heard correctly, Admiral," Ariel said. "Between you and me, however, I have serious doubts about the authenticity of these rumours."

"Such is the way of these things. If we believed every rumour we heard, the Hegemony would be so powerful that they could wipe out all life on Earth without breaking a sweat. If they can even sweat. These

Mages they have, they're powerful, but I can't believe they have that much power at their fingertips or the Empire would have been absorbed at the command of the Hegemon years ago."

Ariel chuckled at the thought, his humour hiding the sudden uncomfortable feeling that had blossomed in his chest. "They aren't that strong, George, that's why we've been offered a seat at the negotiating table – they're testing us and our contest with the Lukratza is just the first step in the process."

"Is it a step the Empire can take? Is it even a step that it wants to take? I know you trust Colonel Brydges, yet I can't help but wonder if he's the right man for the job. Why aren't you the one on the ground?"

"The Lukratza made a request to the Hegemony that high-level commanders be excluded from the Dùbhlan. They agreed. When I got the news, I couldn't figure out why until I realised that they want to test our military as thoroughly as they can – including how capable and adaptable the chain of command is. Do we follow orders blindly no matter what's happening in front of us or do we adapt and overcome?"

Admiral Leystrom turned back to the hologram, the blue illumination from the map giving the man an eerie, haunted look. Motioning with his hands, the projection zoomed in on the soon-to-be headquarters of Colonel Brydges. He stared at it thoughtfully for a few seconds, thinking through the implications of the information that the General had just given him. After a while, he muttered something that Ariel only just caught, "I hope he's up to the challenge."

As do I, thought Ariel, *but at least I have faith that with soldiers like Sergeant Reynolds under his command, Brydges isn't going to cock it up. It'd take a special kind of mistake to mess it up that badly.*

4

CHAPTER FOUR

The loading ramp of the dropship opened at speed, allowing a wave of moist, hot air to waft into the troop compartment. Giving the ramp barely enough time to make contact with the floor, Reynold's squad raced out of the ship, rifles raised and already scanning the dense undergrowth. Johnson and Sinclair went left, allowing Baker and Haley to go right. Close behind them came Reynolds, moving straight out of the bay onto the lush grass of the clearing. He waiting patiently for a report as his squad sprinted across the open area and through into the jungle ahead.

"Clear!" Johnson reported over the comm just before Haley did the same.

"Right, form a perimeter. Baker, get the radio out of the dropship and set it up. Let the Colonel know that we're rolling out the welcome mat. Ask him if he wants to bring the kids along to play." Reynolds circled around the clearing until he was right in front of the dropship, its powerful engines idling as it waited for permission to depart.

"Once that's done, you flyboys can get back to your five-star hotel upstairs. I heard it was Mexican night tonight," he added as an aside, directing the comment to the pilots who had brought them here. His reply from the pilot was the middle finger. Some insults just never grew old and this was a classic.

Baker had returned to the dropship and had lifted the heavy comm gear with some difficulty, only possible because of the power-assisted armour he was wearing. He carried it out and set it down on a bare, dusty patch of land in the middle of the clearing. The landing ramp whirred shut and the dropship fired its engines, gracefully hovering a few metres off the ground before angling up and shooting into the distance. Within seconds, it had dwindled to a small speck – a stark counterpoint to the hundreds of dropships moving in the opposite direction.

"Would you look at that?" Haley said in wonder. "I've never seen that many birds in the air at once. What about you, guys?"

Reynolds stopped cold on his way over to join Baker and glanced up before resuming towards the comm gear. "Yeah, Haley. It doesn't happen often but when it does, it usually means something bad is about to happen."

"You've seen it before, Sarge? When?"

"Don't ask me that again, Haley," a note of anger creeping into his voice. "Do yourself a favour and don't ask anyone that question again. You've no idea the pain it can cause."

#

It's amazing the difference a day can make, Reynolds thought as he marched between numerous tents and pre-fab buildings that had sprung up almost overnight. After securing the area, the Colonel and his command team had swept down into the clearing and transformed it into something approaching civilisation. As he got closer to the tent that was being used as Brydges' Command Information Centre, or CIC, he heard a shout and then a bang, as if something breakable had been thrown.

"What use are tanks in this environment?!" Brydges shouted at a hapless aide who had bent over to clear up the remains of the mug that had been the victim of the Colonel's ire. "It's a Kingdamned jungle! Why in the hell have we been given half a dozen tanks when they can't move more than a few metres before getting stuck in the bloody shrubs?"

The aide finished cleaning the mess and scurried away from the tent, desperate to escape Colonel Brydges and questions he wasn't expected to have the answer to. As his eyes followed the retreating aide, Brydges clocked Reynolds' arrival and glared at him, embarrassed that the Sergeant had witnessed the emotional outburst.

Fighting back a smirk, Reynolds came to a halt in front of the Colonel and snapped a salute. After receiving a salute in return, he said, "The way I see it, sir, there's lots of things you can do with these tanks. Alright, they may not be useful in the conventional sense but if the Lukratza make it this far, they could be invaluable."

"Okay, Sergeant, I'll humour you. Please do tell me how we could use them?" His sarcasm was obvious, his voice dripping with insincerity.

"A couple of things spring to mind, sir. You could remove the turrets from the main body and place them in foxholes around the site, providing you with a hardpoint that can fire nice big shells. Or we could clear the jungle around the campsite for half a klick and provide a stable ground for the tanks to act as a quick reaction force to counter any attacks."

Looking pensive, Brydges took a few seconds to think the suggestions through. He dropped the insincerity from his voice and quickly warmed to Reynolds. "Some good ideas, Sergeant. Care for a place on my staff?"

"Thank you but no thank you, sir. I'm fine with my squad." Reynolds had been given such an offer before but if he wasn't there to look after Johnson, Haley and the gang – hell, even that rookie, Baker – who else would be? They were his team, his family and he would rather be shot than leave them to fend for themselves.

"I understand. Most days, I'd prefer to be back in the field with a squad rather than sat behind a desk working with this bunch of miscreants." The smile on his face showed he meant his words in jest and the answering smile on the faces of his staff told Reynolds that they were used to this. Perhaps the outburst he'd witnessed on his arrival was the anomaly rather than the rule.

Brydges walked away and motioned for Reynolds to follow. "Between you and me, son, I've got a good bunch of good people working for me and you're one of them."

They walked towards the outskirts of the tented village and eventually came to the edge. It was clear that Brydges wanted some privacy and he had to wave two sentries away when they moved to follow. They weren't happy about it but complied, allowing the two men to walk away. Geoff was sure that he could see them following the pair at a discreet distance, still intent on keeping an eye on their charge. When there was no one else in earshot, Colonel Brydges came to a halt and turned to Reynolds.

"Okay, I'm going to level with you. I know I can trust you. I've seen your record and I know that you're a career soldier and that you've earned numerous awards, most of which are classified beyond belief. As much faith as I have in these boys and girls, I'm a little nervous about what's coming. We've known each other a long time, Geoff, and I know I can count on you to do your best to save as many lives as possible."

Reynolds nodded. "Yes, sir. You know I will. What would you have me do?"

"You're going to be my main quick reaction force. I'm giving you a chopper so you can move around the field quickly. I want you monitoring the channels and when we figure out where the main attack will be coming from, or when a section is hard-pressed to keep itself together, I want you and your guys sweeping in like avenging angels. These grunts are going to be looking to you to be their first line of support, so don't let them down." Brydges stopped to see if there was a comment forthcoming. There wasn't, so he continued issuing his orders.

"We've got ten days before the start of the Dùbhlan, as well as this damned drinks reception thing. Make the most of it. Learn the ground and the demarcation lines of the battlefield until you know it like the back of your hand. Where can we fall back to at a pinch… what would work as a good ambush point… suss them all out. You're going to be my eyes and ears and, with any luck, you'll also be the ace up my sleeve."

Oh, nothing difficult then, Reynolds thought. "Yes, sir. Request permission to begin?"

29

"Granted. Keep me posted on your progress and if there's anything you can use, personnel or material, you let me know. I mean it – anything you need, Geoff, I'll make sure you have it quicker than I can issue the orders." With these words, the Colonel about-faced and began the journey back to his CIC. After a couple of steps, he pulled up short and turned back. "Geoff? You take care of your team and, most importantly, yourself. Do you hear me?" He turned and continued on his way without waiting for a reply.

Just before he went out of sight, Reynolds heard him hollering at the top of his voice.

"Gordon! Get some men with big flamethrowers to clear me an exclusion zone half a klick big around the camp! While you're at it, tell those bloody tankers to start dismantling their precious babies and dig some big holes!"

5

Chapter Five

Danny flew through the air and collided with a column that someone had inconveniently placed right in the middle of the testing hall. It wasn't the first time and it wouldn't be the last – regardless of how hard she tried, she could never do anything to please the Lord Regent or her other tutors. As she was only a novice, she had been placed in classes with children much younger than she and her lack of knowledge showed, constantly leaving her at a disadvantage and making her look like an easy target. She had resolved not to show any weakness when in the company of others and, so far, this tactic had been working to her benefit. It was mentally exhausting but Danny thought that she would rather be tired than get bullied by children much younger and vicious than she was.

She slowly picked herself up from the floor, wiping away the blood running from her nose with her sleeve and pulled herself up to her full height. She faced back down the hallway and started glaring daggers at the Lord Regent who stood on a podium at the head of the hall, a conductor controlling the orchestra. He glared back at her and she realised that she had soiled her robe – almost a cardinal sin. It wouldn't matter to the Lord Regent that it wasn't her fault that she had blood on her clothes. She would be pulling double chores tonight.

"Such bravery will serve you well, should you ever become proficient enough in Magick to be useful," he said with a sneer.

Oh, how she hated that man, with his bald, shiny head and arrogant face.

"Come back here and sit in your place. Quickly now."

Danny moved back towards the group of students, at this stage in their training referred to as neophytes, assembled in front of the Lord Regent and sat on the cold, hard marble floor. She stared ahead, ignoring the snickers and looks of disgust that came from her classmates. They really detested her, thinking that she always got special attention from the tutors when, in fact, the opposite was true. Her face burned red with shame and hot tears gathered in her eyes. She attempted to reassert control by breathing slowly, calming herself down whilst vowing to never repeat the mistake she had just made. She would learn from this and come back stronger.

"As I was saying," the Lord Regent carried on as if nothing had happened, "Some of you are getting to the stage where you will be trusted to take short journeys out of the Citadel alongside some of your more educated colleagues. You will all be aware that the Dùbhlan begins tomorrow, and as we are the caretakers of this planet, it falls to us to preside over the contest, a fact that we are proud of. A fact that you would do well not to mar."

Danny felt a wave of revulsion rise within her chest. This contest was despicable, pitting intelligent people against one another for nothing but honour and entertainment. Surely a truly civilised society could come up with better ways to solve their problems?

Not missing the wave of emotion coming from the students, the Lord Regent's eyes turned hard. "Some of you clearly disapprove. Yes, it is cruel. You must, however, use your heads. This competition has taken the place of regular warfare. How many more people would die in a normal war? How many men, women, children – families of innocents?"

His obvious hypocrisy made Danny sick. She knew that he wasn't above killing innocents – all she had to do to prove it was close her eyes and listen to her family being murdered again.

32

The Lord Regent moved away from the podium and began pacing around the edge of the group, all the while continuing his tirade.

"It is our duty, amongst others, to ensure that both sides in the Dùbhlan play by the rules – our rules. Equal levels of technology, blanket refusal on the use of chemical, biological or nuclear weapons. Most importantly – no Magick. That is, unless we ourselves choose to use it in the execution of our duties."

Arriving back at the front of the group, he once again took his place at the podium. He cast his eye and his mind over the group, taking note of those whose robes were being worn incorrectly or were dirty, those whose Magickal potential barely flickered within them. *All except her*, he thought, *yet none of them can see it bar me. I must make my stamp on this child and ensure that if anyone can influence her in the future, it is me.*

"The reason we are gathered here is simple. Behind you is the Citadel Rock." He pointed over their heads and the entire class eagerly turned to look. Hovering in an alcove to one side of the room was a perfectly smooth boulder, gleaming in the near darkness that seemed to be cloaking it. Danny spent a short time trying to figure out how it was kept in place and then mentally ticked herself off. The obvious answer was Magick and she was frustrated that it had taken her so long to arrive at that conclusion considering where she was.

It was large, approximately twelve feet in diameter and seemed to hum quietly, a background noise that couldn't be ignored no matter how hard one tried. Danny listened intently to the susurrus and thought that it sounded similar to a household vacuum cleaner. The stone itself was made from pure flint, one of the strongest natural substances and was worn away from innumerable children and youngsters running their fingers along the smooth face.

"Countless generations of Mages have tried to remove the stone from the field holding it in place. Each and every one of them failed. Only one has had even an ounce of success – me. Alas, I could not remove it completely from the field but the Order had to acknowledge my power when I made it move."

Danny felt his enjoyment at that, the thought that only he had been strong enough. He was too much in love with himself she decided, then quickly became fascinated with the surface of the Rock, hoping that the Lord Regent hadn't caught her thought.

"One by one you will attempt to move the Rock. Should you succeed, you will be coupled up with a Mage for the rest of your training and sent out to participate in the Dùbhlan. Should you fail?" Danny sensed the enjoyment grow stronger - "Fail and you will be…disposed of."

#

It wasn't fair! Danny looked around at her classmates in shock as they began excitedly whispering to each other after the Lord Regent's announcement. All the others had been raised in the Citadel, taken as babies and trained how to use Magick. In contrast, Danny herself had only been here for a few short weeks and now she was expected to do something that was supposed to be difficult for people with years more experience than she had under her belt.

She was afraid. It sat heavy in her stomach, making her feel sick. She looked up at the Lord Regent and saw him watching her, that irritating half-smile perpetually on his face. As she noticed him and their eyes made contact, the heat of anger crept in and began to slowly replace the cold, paralysing fear. She flexed her fingers and felt the heat spread throughout her body until she felt as if she were ablaze, revelling in the comfort that the fire seemed to bring her.

The assembled youngsters, all from a variety of species, began to line up in front of the Rock with the Lord Regent taking his place next to it. The children were almost fighting for places, the more confident ones placing themselves at the front and the ones like Danny, terrified out of their minds, jostling to go last. Danny received a kick in the shins and an elbow in the ribs as she finally found a place near the back. She would be second to last to go but at least she hadn't been made to bleed again.

"Begin," The Lord Regent commanded without any further ado. The first neophyte waltzed up to the Rock. He wasn't of a species that Danny was familiar with, looking like a cross between cow and bear. He was taller than she and she knew from watching him these past few weeks that he was one of the most talented in the Citadel. He knew it too and it showed in the way he carried himself, rarely deigning to even acknowledge the other neophytes.

He began to focus, screwing his bovine face up with intense concentration. Nothing happened at first but after a few seconds, the Rock moved an inch to the side as if struck by a hammer.

"Good. You have passed. Next." There was no note of encouragement or congratulation in the Lord Regent's voice, simply boredom. The neophyte sighed in relief and walked to the side, crossing his arms as he prepared to watch his colleagues go through their own personal tests. The second student walked forward and looked at the Rock, her face looking almost identical to the bovine-like student who had been successful only moments before.

Another pass and another student sighing in relief. A short nod from the Lord Regent showed his approval and then yet another student took the step forward, this one obviously shaking with fear.

Danny lost interest after the first few attempts from her classmates. She was so consumed with worry about her turn, she barely noticed when a neophyte closer to the front lost his nerve and tried to run. He raced away from the Rock, moving towards the large entrance to the Hall. He didn't make it. The Lord Regent looked at him with disappointment, then raised a hand and clicked his fingers. The boy burst into flames. The class could only stare as the boy began to scream, letting the pain tear out into the open with his voice until, after an agonisingly long minute, he went quiet and dropped to the floor. Not a single one of them moved to help – nor would they have been able to do anything if they had.

35

"A shame. Poor Seamus would have made a good Mage if only his heart were in it."

Desperately trying to ignore the sight of Seamus' remains and block the smell of burning flesh from her mind, Danny's anger grew again. It was a horrible way to die but no one would ever hold the Lord Regent accountable – and he had done it as an example.

Two places from the front now, Danny tried to calm down. She reached into herself and tried to find that elusive feeling, that little nub in her brain that would help her to control Magick. It was one of the first lessons that children were taught at the Citadel and it had been surprisingly easy for Danny to master.

Okay, I can do this, I can do this. What am I thinking? I can't do this! She started hyperventilating, a mild panic attack almost pushing her to run like Seamus had. The memory of his burning flesh swept across her nostrils and steeled her nerves.

"Your turn next, orphan," the neophyte behind her gave her a push. "Don't die. We'd all hate it if we had to do your chores on top of our own."

Danny was shocked to see that she was now at the front. To the side stood all the neophytes who had passed the test, staring back at the remaining children as if eager to see someone else fail. *This is it. Do or die.* She stepped up and looked the Lord Regent straight in one of his verdant green eyes.

He leaned in, whispering words that only she could hear. "Farewell, child. For the short time I knew you, you were constantly a disappointment. I can only hope that your parents did not think as little of you as I did, for their sakes."

Choking back furious tears, Danny turned to face the Rock. She took a deep breath, found that intransigent little nub again and pushed through its resistance. She had it! She focused the power onto the Rock, trying to hammer it out of the way as the others had done. It wasn't moving! She increased the pressure and strained her body along with it, willing the Rock to move just a little… until she fell back, exhausted. She'd failed.

The Lord Regent grinned, satisfied with the result. "As I thought. Say farewell to your classmates at once. I said that I would not be giving you a second chance and it seems that your time amongst us is over."

That grin, that awful grin! She abhorred it. It was constantly there, always mocking her, telling her she wasn't good enough. The anger within her chest grew stronger, all-consuming.

"NO!" She screamed and the Magick took over.

The Rock flew out of its place, barrelling at speed towards the Lord Regent. He ducked to narrowly avoid being crushed, then turned to follow the flight of the Rock. It smashed into the podium, causing bits of wood to go flying everywhere before hitting the wall behind and cracking into two large pieces, a few smaller ones spinning away across the marble floor.

A stunned silence reigned over the room. Danny wiped tears of anger away from her eyes and faced the Lord Regent where he lay on the ground, wondering what punishment would be in store for her for breaking the Rock.

The Lord Regent slowly came to himself and looked at Danny. It was the first time he had looked at her without that mocking smile. In its place was something she had never thought to see - fear.

6

CHAPTER SIX

Mage Rhiannon clapped her hands together and strode forward with a sense of purpose. Danny followed meekly, still not accustomed to the respect being shown by her new mentor or even the fact that she had been assigned to a Master. It had happened rapidly after her test at the Citadel.

She had been separated from her classmates quicker than she could blink and confined to a cell at the bottom of the tower with no explanation. She wasn't mistreated; she had only been confined in the small, dark room for her own protection. Those were the words that they had used when she demanded an explanation but she didn't believe it at first. She could feel the fear coming from the guards and she didn't understand.

Although the cell had been as far from the common areas of the Citadel as it was possible to be, she was surprised to have been able to feel the Mages' emotions swirling around like a thick, early morning fog from her cot. She couldn't know the exact distance but it seemed that by using the Magick in such a strong outburst, she had increased her power and made it possible to sense the torrent. Maybe it was always the same, maybe when you used Magick you became stronger, or maybe it was because she was getting used to the little voice whispering in her head, beginning to accept it like a friend despite the obvious problems that came with it. She only hoped that she would be strong enough not to get swept up in the river of power that threatened to overtake her.

The bare, aged stone of the cell wall was becoming ever more fascinating for her, trapped as she was with no distraction. She started counting a slow drip coming from the single, barred window set deep in the wall, fighting to stay awake. The dark thoughts stayed with her, keeping her company through the isolation. The Magick was whispering louder here as there was nothing to drown it out and she hallucinated that she was holding a conversation with it.

It was telling her that she could do anything if only they worked together. She was sure that the voice wasn't really there but it sounded clearly as if it were someone talking over her shoulder. It was hard to ignore the tone of the voice, its sweetness worming its way through her mind until she found herself agreeing readily. She twisted on the cot, looking for the source of the voice before dismissing it as a phantasm. She had gone her entire life without hearing this voice and now she accepted it as the norm despite it being something that would have had her confined to a mental institution had she mentioned this to her parents back on Earth.

Was she going insane? It was hard to tell and so she hesitantly turned her attention to something that she could understand only a little better, allowing the emotions from the others to roll through her. With the voice relegated to the background – now almost shouting for her attention but getting nothing back – she slowly began to unravel the mystery of her captivity.

She could tell that the entire Order was arguing amongst itself about what her test meant, about what they should do with her. The emotions were running hot throughout the complex and it bled down to her cell. She slowly became more worried and desperate, imagining the worst-case scenarios and playing them through to the end. Inevitably, none of them ended well for her. Eventually, she had felt the anger being replaced with acceptance and she began to hope that her ordeal was almost over. Surely that was a good thing? Only time would tell.

#

She hadn't felt them approaching the cell, the Masters shielding their thoughts from her and keeping her on edge for a little longer. She had been given to Mage Rhiannon, a respected and wizened master of the Order who had comforted her and reassured her that everything was going to be okay. She gave no explanation about what had happened above, or even of what the outcome of her test meant. What she had done was provide her with a sense of safety and security that she hadn't felt since she'd been abducted from her family on Earth.

"I am Mage Rhiannon. You will address me as Master so long as you are with me," she had said. "You have been apprenticed to me for the rest of your training. The Order doesn't normally pair Apprentices with Masters of their own species but yours is a... special case and the Council thought I had much to offer you. I have no doubt that in years to come, it will be me calling you Master."

She had smiled at Danny and she sensed the genuine warmth behind the woman's demure façade. It was a different type of heat from the clash of emotions from earlier, this one almost like sitting by an open fire in the depths of winter rather than a raging torrent of a house fire. She reminded Danny of her mother, a not unpleasant familiarity that put her at ease.

"Yes, Master. What will my training entail? When do we get started?"

"Bold. Seemingly without fear and still to learn some manners, I see. That will come with time. Very well. I'll explain some more for you, seeing as that brute doesn't seem to have done it himself. What he was thinking, taking you from your family the way he did, I'll never know."

"That brute?" Danny whispered, knowing that Rhiannon was talking about the Lord Regent and was afraid that he might overhear. She had never heard any of the others say a bad word about the man and realised that she was in the presence of a supremely confident woman.

"The Lord Regent is skilled, ambitious and ruthless. He has no qualms in eliminating any perceived threat to his stature. You would do well not to draw his attention to you any further." Rhiannon smiled again, nullifying the threat in her words. "Never repeat what I just said to anyone else. You may find the result to be unpleasant." She winked and Danny suppressed a giggle. She could tell that she was going to get on with her Master.

"To answer your question, your training will involve spending a lot of time with me. I'll be teaching you how to better tap into that Magickal reserve in your mind that allows you to manipulate space, time and objects. You'll learn how to speak telepathically, move objects precisely and even transmute matter from one form to another amongst other things. It will involve a lot of time and patience but I dare say that you are the most talented being to come through the Citadel in my lifetime – if not anyone's lifetime."

The words left Danny speechless, wondering what it was that she had done to deserve such a possibility. She vowed to make the most of it, the determination seeping out of her giving Rhiannon a good look at the inner workings of her new apprentice. If nothing else, she would have wanted to make her parents proud.

#

That evening, barely hours after meeting Rhiannon for the first time, her Master led the way towards a mixed group of beings, all of whom held an alcoholic beverage in their hands as they mingled and negotiated final details. The setting sun of Midway cast golden rays through the open space, highlighting the liquid falling from elaborate water fountains and giving an ethereal cast to the assembled peoples.

There were representatives from nearly all races in the Hegemony as well as a sparse number from without – various insect-types, lizard-types, even some floating bag-like beings who normally dwelt in gas giants on the periphery of star systems. Danny had been told by Rhiannon in the short time before this event that those beings who lived in the gas giants very rarely left the sanctuary of their homeworlds, taking only the most exciting opportunities to interact physically with their galactic neighbours.

Danny gasped as she nearly put her foot down on something that looked like a snake, muttering an apology to the being without knowing if it would understand her. The being glared at her and then took off quickly towards two larger versions of itself. When it got to them, it coiled itself around the midsection of the larger being – Danny realised that they must be its parents and she had nearly trodden on a child!

Her attention came back to the menagerie of beings having the time of their lives and was starting to commit it all to memory, promising herself that she would never forget this moment.

So many different people! Danny had never seen anything like it and her head was on a swivel, trying to take in as much as possible as they moved. Before her abduction, she had never seen anything other than a human and was delighted at the opportunity to see so many socialising in harmony.

The Dùbhlan was of such importance to the Hegemony and the peoples therein that the start of each one was heralded as a public holiday. People would dance, drink and fuck like it was going out of fashion, crazed in their debauchery. Once the contest began, they would go back to their normal working lives but would huddle around their equivalent of a television screen each night to see the scores or watch it live on screens in entertainment establishments. *Not the scores*, Danny reminded herself, *the casualty reports*. This thought brought her head out of the clouds and she remembered that they were here to celebrate a war.

A clear, piercing note sounded from a brass bell and all attention turned to a stage that had been set up in the courtyard, backdropped by the impressive and intimidating construction of the Citadel. Standing at the front of the swollen crowd was a Kir'archi, an insectoid race typically found in administrative positions in the Hegemony. He (Danny assumed it was a he) began making odd clicking noises that seemed to be making sense to the assembled people.

Danny didn't understand a word of what the Kir'archi was saying and looked at Rhiannon, hoping for a translation. Rhiannon reached into one of the numerous pockets in her robe and drew out a small hunk of metal, mentally berating herself for not thinking of doing it sooner. She handed it to Danny and motioned to her ear, clearly instructing her on what to do. Once the device was in place, Danny gasped as a toneless, neutral voice began translating everything the Kir'archi was saying.

"Ladies and Gentlemen, boys and girls of all races and ages! Welcome to the six hundred and forty-third Dùbhlan!" A cheer swelled from the crowd. "We have an incredible match-up for you this year. The newcomers, all the way from Earth – the British Empire!"

Only a few people cheered for that, Danny included. She noticed that most of those doing so were humans with only a smattering of others taking part. The Empire was clearly not popular in the Hegemony and it was little wonder – there had essentially been a cold war between the two powers for decades. She wondered what propaganda was broadcast by the Hegemony and then decided that she really did not want to know.

"Facing off against them are the returning champions. You know them – you love them – the Lukratza!"

This time, the noise was overwhelming. It seemed like everyone was supporting the Lukratza, perhaps hopeful that the favourites would win again. Danny wondered how many of them had bet against her people. She dreaded looking at the inevitable images of dead humans that the news programmes were sure to include in their reports but somehow thought that would only make the majority of beings happy.

7

CHAPTER SEVEN

He really hated these things. Any sort of social engagement outside of the military drove John Brydges into fight or flight mode, except he could never actually get out of the damned things. He would endure although he really wasn't happy about it. Although he was excited about the opening of the contest, he was really looking forward to the end of the party and the start of battle. *There's something you don't hear every day*, he mused.

He'd brought some of his command staff with him, with the addition of Sergeant Reynolds and his squad, hoping that together they could try and gain some insight into the Lukratza's game plan. Not that he was an expert at reading alien body language but it didn't hurt to try. Anything they gleaned could be crucial down the line and he was committed to doing as much right by his troops as he could.

He heard the sound of human laughter ahead and followed it quickly to the source. Reynolds was the cause – by the look of it, he'd just finished telling a joke to his squad. Private Baker had found it so funny he'd thrown his drink all over Private Haley and she was giving him a smack on the back of his head as a prize. Brydges smiled to himself, all hope that his soldiers would behave themselves whilst in public going out of the window.

"Care to share?" He chimed in when the revelries had subsided. The soldiers snapped to attention when they saw who had spoken. Brydges waved at them. "Stand easy, guys. It's a party, not a parade."

"Sir, I was just telling them about the time you pulled my arse out of the fire at Pollux – literally!" Reynolds sounded sheepish, unsure about telling this anecdote now that one of the main characters was present – and a superior at that.

Sergeant Reynolds (then Corporal) had been in the same battalion as Colonel Brydges (then Lieutenant) during an engagement around the star of Pollux. The Empire had been expanding rapidly and bullying nearby governments to try to get away with it. Swiftly taking control of a lot of real estate close to Earth, it wasn't long before they were butting heads with civilisations that had already laid claim to planets along the coreward path. There wasn't a lot of land up for grabs in a rapidly shrinking galaxy and conflict was inevitable; the royal forces were soon earning their pay. Using a strike-first tactic, they had been able to secure multiple star systems without too many casualties; thinking that it had worked in the past, the King had greedily pushed his forces further and faster with each passing year.

Unfortunately for the men and women involved, at Pollux, the Kir'archi had pushed back. They didn't take kindly to the pressure being brought to bear on them and it was a stroke of luck that they decided to handle the matter themselves rather than involve the Hegemony. It said a lot about how little the assembled races thought of the Empire that the Kir'archi, not a militarily inclined species, thought that they would be able to win the day without any outside assistance.

Pollux was one of their primary breeding grounds, something that the Royal Intelligence Corps hadn't thought to mention to the Generals when they made their move on the system. The Royal fleet had swept in and pacified the minimal amount of resistance that the Kir'archi fleet had put up. The bugs weren't known for the prowess of their navy, preferring for the Lukratza to do the heavy lifting for them instead. So far so good, all going according to plan. They weren't prepared for what would happen on the ground, however. The events that would follow would embed themselves permanently into the human psyche and was taught to young children as the prime example of hubris.

There was a protracted ground war on the only habitable planet in the system, with wave after wave of reinforcements being shipped in from Earth. The Kir'archi were simply too determined not to lose such a precious plot of land and they did the same, ship after ship arriving from their colonies to keep the pressure on the humans. In the final confrontation in the conflict, Reynolds had been captured. His company had been tasked with capturing a communications station and the assault started promisingly. After allowing the human company to take the station with little opposition, the Kir'archi had sprung their trap and decimated the human forces, leaving a wounded but still combat-capable Reynolds to take on a regiment of Kir'archi almost single-handedly.

The Kir'archi had been so impressed when they had finally nullified Reynolds' surviving troops, they'd trussed him up and started cooking him over an open fire – their way of honouring a worthy foe. Luckily for Reynolds, Brydges had ignored orders and taken a team in to rescue him only moments before Reynolds' bare arse was lowered onto the flames. Reynolds had never forgotten that Brydges had risked his life and career to save him and strived to repay him at every opportunity. It had been a very productive working relationship.

Brydges joined in with the renewed laughter. The sight of Reynolds tied up like a pig on a spit had stuck with him and made him chuckle whenever he thought of it. "I've just thought of something, Sergeant. Why don't you rename your squad the Flaming Donkeys in honour of your greatest achievement?"

The squad was uncontrollable at this, both the alcohol and the joke conspiring to make the situation even funnier. Brydges received a sharp look from Reynolds, telling him he would pay for it later, ranks notwithstanding.

"Come on, Geoff. We've been summoned by the powers that be." Brydges quickly changed the subject, hoping that by doing so he would make Reynolds forget his quip.

"By name, sir? Didn't think I rated high enough on the list to receive an official invitation."

"You don't but I do and if I've got to go meet the enemy, I want to make damn sure you're by my side. Besides, you're a seasoned veteran."

"I swear, I'm gonna slap you...sir."

8

CHAPTER EIGHT

"Welcome, honourable beings. Can I provide either of you with any refreshments?" The Kir'archi who had spoken moved over to a darker corner of the luxuriously decorated conference room and swung open the doors of a well-stocked drinks cabinet, waiting for an answer. The way he was moving his multiple limbs was jerky and so against what the humans were used to seeing that it instinctively set the two men on edge. A glass ceiling allowed the starlight to filter into the room now that the sun had set, making the Kir'archi's movements even more unnerving.

"Coffee would be grand if you have any," Brydges answered for the Sergeant as well. Both he and Reynolds made their way over to the conference table that dominated the centre of the room and they fell gratefully into their seats, pleased to be away from the crowded party going on outside. The Kir'archi closed the drinks cabinet and began making the hot drinks. As he did so, he continued talking to them.

"My name is Kir'ami and I am the official representative of the Hegemon himself for the duration of the Dùbhlan. I've organised this meeting between you and the Lukratza commander to make sure we are all in agreement over the rules and regulations under which you will be fighting." Kir'ami looked at the medals displayed prominently on Brydges' dress uniform. "Such an esteemed commander as yourself should have no difficulties in meeting the enemy face to face, I assume?"

The need to reply was negated as the door to the room swung open once more. Reynolds found himself tensing his body in preparation for a fight as the Lukratza commander waltzed in with an air of disinterest – not an easy task considering the size of him.

"Ah, Commander. Welcome."

The Lukratza nodded at Kir'ami, snapping his teeth together as he did so, and then moved to stand behind the opposite side of the table to the two soldiers. A strange, musky smell had followed the lizard into the room and Reynolds coughed in reaction, something that the Commander didn't miss. Reynolds went bright red and nodded at the Lukratza once in greeting but received no reply. After making sure that Reynolds knew he was being eyeballed, the Lukratza returned to ignoring the two humans. He didn't sit down but instead stood there whilst swinging his tail laconically behind him, the full force of his attention now on the Kir'archi who had finished making the coffee.

"I'm here, Kir'ami. What do you want?"

"As I was just saying to these two gentlebeings, the Hegemon just wants to make sure we all understand one another. Please sit."

"I will not. Get on with it." The Commander bared his teeth at Kir'ami to accentuate his comment and the insectoid wisely did not press the issue. He passed the two mugs of steaming coffee over to the humans and took his place at the head of the table.

"Very well. As you all know, there are certain rules and regulations that must be followed. Aside from all the obvious ones, such as no chemical, biological or nuclear weapons, no cheating and no Magick, we must agree on the maximum technology levels used by both sides."

The Colonel was troubled and furrowed his brow in thought. Something about this didn't feel right to him – hadn't they already agreed to this some months before embarking on the journey to Midway? Why decide now? *I wonder if the Lukratza have brought weapons and technology with them that we can't compete against*, he thought. Looking at Kir'ami, he thought that the insectoid looked distinctly uncomfortable.

"Why are we having this conversation now, only hours before we begin?" he said, pointedly looking at Kir'ami until the insectoid had to break eye contact. Brydges marvelled that he had just won a staring contest with a being that had four times as many eyes as he did. Another accomplishment to add to his record.

Kir'ami looked to the Lukratza commander who nodded at him with an air of boredom. The Commander was now intently inspecting his talons, flicking imaginary dirt in a display of arrogance that the humans had been expecting and had prepared for.

The insectoid turned back to the humans and rubbed his mandibles together. Brydges wasn't as proficient at reading alien body language as he perhaps ought to be but he knew enough to notice the bug was afraid – not of him but of the Lukratza.

"We are having this conversation now because the Hegemon has decreed that there is to be a... slight change in the pre-agreed rules," Kir'ami said with a grimace as if the words tasted foul in his mouth. "And not in your favour, Colonel. You know of the impeccable and unmatched reputation of the Lukratza, I presume?"

Brydges nodded and glanced at Reynolds out of the corner of his eye. He had a feeling that he knew where this was going and he wasn't happy. He knew that Geoff would be taking this much worse than he was and would be fuming. He just hoped that the other man was keeping his emotions off his face.

"Then you'll know that the only reason we keep the masses under our, that is to say, the Hegemon's control is the threat of direct retribution by the Lukratza. The public knows that if they put a toe (or similar appendage) out of line, the hardest and most severe punishment will be visited upon them by a race not known for its kindness or willingness to negotiate."

Brydges sat forward in his chair, clasping his hands underneath his chin and resting his elbows on the cold surface of the table. "Are you telling me that the Hegemon is so scared of his own population that he rules through fear? We've been told for years that all of the races in the Hegemony live together in harmony, following laws set down by an enlightened government working closely with the Hegemon. You blast it out for all to hear, believing your own propaganda. Is this a lie?" He feigned an innocent tone to try and put Kir'ami off guard.

"It is indeed. The Hegemon rules with an iron fist cloaked in a velvet glove, so to speak. Quite a peculiar adage of your own people, I believe, but an apt one." Kir'ami was twitching noticeably now, the severity of which was increasing the longer this conversation continued.

"Why are you telling me this? Surely you must know that as soon as I report this conversation to my superiors, our news networks will have a field day with this information? What would then happen to your precious Hegemony, your rules and regulations?" Brydges cast an eye over Kir'ami and the Lukratza commander and realised that he hadn't even been given a name for the hulking behemoth of a lizard.

Kir'ami stopped twitching and focused completely on the humans, the threat from the Colonel having the opposite effect to the desired one. "I'm telling you this because you need to know what's in store for you. For the sake of fairness, as much as I can give you. I don't think you'll be putting this in your report, no matter how much you may want to."

"Why the fuck not?" Reynolds looked pissed off and couldn't contain his outburst, speaking for the first time since the meeting began. "You've handed us the perfect weapon with which to reduce your civilisation to a bunch of separate races working against each other. The potential benefits to the Empire are huge and we would be fools not to take advantage. Why are you so confident that we won't use it?"

"Because, petulant child of a human, I have been authorised to make the following statement; if a single word of this goes anywhere other than this conference room, the Hegemony will begin a full-scale war against your Empire. You may believe that you can hold us off for a time but we have resources and technology that are beyond your backwards worlds. As for the Hegemony, you would actually be doing us a favour – nothing unites a people like a common enemy that threatens nothing but destruction."

The room fell silent. Brydges looked outwardly calm but inside, he was furiously working through the problem from every possible angle. His quick mind went through all the possible permutations of what could happen in a matter of seconds and dismissed the ones that made no sense to him. He knew that Reynolds would be doing the same and would be drawing very similar conclusions.

Changing his approach, he looked up at the room and said, "In that case, you can count on our discretion. Yet, you still haven't answered my original question. Why. Are. You. Telling. Us. This?" The last was spoken through gritted teeth.

Kir'ami seemed amused by the Colonel's anger, a stark counterpoint to the anxiety that he had been displaying earlier. Brydges wondered how much of it had been for show. "It works two ways, actually. We've established that the Hegemony would be able to defeat the Empire with minimal effort should it choose to, yes?"

Both Brydges and Reynolds reluctantly nodded their agreement, the admission not sitting well with either of them. They picked up on Kir'ami's qualifier of *should it choose to,* neither of them liking that the insectoid felt secure enough to say it out loud. The Lukratza commander still said nothing, clearly preferring to allow Kir'ami to deal with the situation. It was either that or he genuinely didn't care about this meeting.

"That means we come to the real reason you're here. I am to tell you that you will be allowed to use every weapon at your disposal should you wish, bar the obvious exceptions, as, I'm afraid, are the Lukratza."

#

Both men stormed out of the room after that announcement from Kir'ami, Reynolds calling for transport to take them back to headquarters. Brydges felt a pit in his stomach, made worse by the gloating look the Lukratza commander had on his face when they left. Neither of them spoke to the other as they marched at speed towards the spaceport attached to the facility where the party had only just started in honour of the Dùbhlan. The dark sky and faint starlight gave an eerie aspect to their walk, as if the planet was aware of what was going to happen on its surface and was actively mocking the humans.

Arriving at the port, their bird was already waiting for them on the tarmac with its engines idling. With no need to go through any security, they quickly made their way over to the helicopter and entered, taking their seats in the passengers' compartment without a word. After ensuring that the two VIPs were strapped in, the pilot requested permission to take off from flight control and received it instantly. The chopper began to vibrate as the blades above increased their speed and the engine strained to lift the lifeless metal weight off the ground.

Brydges reached for a comm set and placed it over his head, waiting for Reynolds to do the same. When he had done so, and without preamble, Reynolds said, "We're screwed, sir."

Still angry from the revelations that Kir'ami had shocked them with, Brydges didn't reply straight away, his mind churning through plans and backup plans, anything to find a way out of the situation.

"No, we're not. We've got something the Lukratza don't – you, Geoff. Your role in this is more important than ever. You need to be on top of your game. If you perform as brilliantly as you normally do, we have a chance."

"Permission to speak freely?"

"Granted."

"Weren't you listening to Kir'ami? The Lukratza get to use all their latest technology. The Hegemony has set us up to lose and to lose quickly." Reynolds wasn't holding back now. "Didn't you hear the rumours that the reporting drones are being ordered to ignore any use of technology by the Lukratza that is more advanced than ours? I thought it was bullshit until Kir'ami said what he did. They need the Lukratza to win this because if they don't, every race that has the slightest grudge against

53

them will be spoiling for a fight and the Empire could suddenly find itself in a hot war against a civilisation that could wipe it out."

The chopper sped away from the spaceport and Brydges found that he didn't have a reply.

9

CHAPTER NINE

Danny was standing at the window in her new personal chamber when the Dùbhlan commenced. She had been lost in thought, unaware of the time and was simply staring through the glass at the majestic jungle below when a single red flare rose from the canopy. It arced high into the sky, almost high enough to come in line with her head and then fell gracefully back down to the ground. No sooner had it landed than the gunfire began. *Red for blood*, she thought, *and blood has begun to spill*. She didn't know if that thought had come from her or from the Magick that was still whispering to her.

She still felt uncomfortable in her new blue robe and reached up to her head, pushing back some golden locks that kept escaping her ponytail. The robe was slightly too big for her, having been designed for older and larger apprentices but she liked the way she looked in it. The one chance she had had to look in a mirror had made her smile, knowing that the robe played a big part in making her feel more like an apprentice and less like a helpless victim of the events that had overtaken her life. She also liked that the blue was very similar to the colour of her eyes.

Turning away from the window, she started towards the door to her room but stumbled as a flash of pain swept through her mind, blinding her with its ferocity. Falling lifelessly to the floor, she spent an eternity writhing in agony as pain rampaged through her chest and extremities, struggling to breathe as the pressure in her head increased until she was sure it would explode.

Master Rhiannon burst through the door and came charging into Danny's room. She knelt at Danny's side and placed her hands on either side of the girl's head. Her cold fingers gave Danny the barest second of relief until the pain came sweeping back in like a curtain descending on a stage. Taking a second to gather herself, Rhiannon thrust her thoughts into Danny's mind and spoke.

It's not real! It's not your pain! You have to build a barrier – imagine a wall and focus in on the bricks to the exclusion of all else. I'm shielding you for the moment but I can't keep it up for long. I have to maintain the barriers in my own mind, lest we both end up flopping around on the floor like fish out of water.

Danny gnashed her teeth together in pain and tried to picture a wall. For a few desperate seconds, she was unable to do so until she thought of her parents. Their smiling faces floated in her mind's eye and she focused on them. She had loved them so much and still experienced the initial pain and loss on a daily basis.

The pain began to subside and Danny was able to think more clearly. Realising that thoughts of her parents were helping, she remembered the many happy days she'd had with them, the family picnics and trips out. The dinners together and the many birthday parties they had thrown for her. The pain lessened further and she found she was able to sit up, supported by Rhiannon.

"What was that?" Danny asked when she had caught her breath. On her way down, she had knocked a chair to the ground and had been awkwardly sprawled across it, as the ache in her muscles now attested. It had never crossed her mind that she had made a symbolic wall of memories rather than that of a physical construct.

"Those, my dear, were echoes of the trials that the soldiers in the jungle below are going through at this very minute. I know that you are aware that the Magick can allow you to feel the emotions of those around you but I should have remembered to tell you that it has another effect, one far less pleasant. You can feel their pain, Danny, as if it were your own. It is a burden that we all have to bear, a price to pay for the gifts we have been given."

Rhiannon smiled kindly at her before continuing yet Danny thought that she looked sad. "The Dùbhlan is a testing time for many in the Order not just because we have to watch so many people die but because we have to feel it. It is one of the hardest things I have ever had to do and for not preparing you, I sincerely apologise."

Rhiannon helped Danny to sit on her bed and checked her over. "You've got a cut on your head. You must be one of the clumsiest children I've ever met. You always seem to be bleeding!"

Danny laughed, the happiness going through her causing the pain being forced on her to retreat even further. Rhiannon sat next to the child, her quiet companionship allowing Danny to gather her thoughts. For a few minutes, they just sat there and Rhiannon waited patiently for the girl to speak her mind.

Eventually, Danny quietly said, "I couldn't picture a wall, Master. I pictured my parents instead. Even though they aren't here anymore, they're still helping me. I miss them a lot. I think they would have liked you, Master." Her voice trailed off at the end and she resumed staring into space, lost in her own head.

Not allowing it to show on her face, Rhiannon felt a sense of immense pride in Danny, concurrently empathising with the guilt and fear that the girl must be feeling. She was only a child but she was already mature beyond her years. For someone so young to have gone through so much in less than thirteen years of life… it was criminal.

This one was going to be formidable; Rhiannon could tell. Time, training and experience would change her from a gangly teenager into a respected Mage. She looked forward to seeing the transformation. She cast her thoughts back to what the Lord Regent had said to her when she had volunteered to mentor and care for the child. *Can this child really be what we have been looking for after all these years?*

#

A bandage now installed around her wounded head, courtesy of one of the nurses who lived in the compound, Danny followed Rhiannon to the mess hall. She felt like she was always following the gentle Master everywhere but knew that was only because she didn't really know her way around the Citadel yet. She didn't mind though. Rhiannon was so unlike the horrible Lord Regent in so many ways. She was kind and seemed to understand what Danny was going through. She promised herself that she would never let the older woman down.

They approached two large wooden doors at the end of the stone corridor which led through to the mess hall. The entrance was guarded by two apprentices, both of whom were wearing blue robes. Robe colour seemed to signify rank, Danny realised, with white for neophytes, blue for apprentices, green for Mages and red for Masters. Presumably, the black robes that the Lord Regent wore were for him alone, another way for the man to express his belief that he was above the rest of the Order. She wondered why the doors needed guarding in the first place then pushed the thought to the back of her mind, aware of the need to keep an eye on where she was going.

As they entered the mess hall, a wall of noise and an assortment of smells hit them. It seemed like every member of the order who wasn't actively involved in the Dùbhlan had gathered in this one place to keep updated on the contest. Large vidscreens had been placed at regular intervals around the room, all of them showing the footage from the Hegemony's dedicated news and sports channel. Students were gathered in groups comparing what looked like scorecards and numerous beings from multiple races were wearing either the British coat of arms or the Hegemony's symbol on their sleeves, showing their support for either side like fans at a football match.

58

Although she wanted to look around and investigate the scene of revelry, Rhiannon was heading straight through the throng towards a smaller room set off the side and Danny didn't want to be left alone with her peers, not yet. She still hadn't forgiven them for the strongly negative emotions that many of them had felt towards her during the previously unexplained incarceration.

Despite the hall being so packed, the Mages seemed to be giving the door to this room a wide berth, perhaps respectful of what was happening inside. This time, the two apprentices flanking this door challenged them, taking their duties more seriously than the other two. Rhiannon produced a datapad from within her voluminous robes and flashed it at the apprentices. Looking cowed, they bowed their heads and opened the door for Rhiannon and Danny to move through. As she went past, Danny smiled at them and received a shy smile back as her reward. Maybe she could begin to forgive some of them, especially the really cute one on the left.

Standing in the small room that they entered was the Lord Regent and Danny's mood dropped once again. After the last few days, he was the last person that she wanted to see. She would have to get used to seeing him though, considering he was in charge of the Order. The curtains were drawn over the windows, leaving the room dark and feeling like it was underground. Was the dread that Danny had felt on her approach to the room caused by the Dùbhlan or from the man now staring at her? She looked at the Lord Regent and thought that he looked even more pale and sickly in this lighting than he had before.

"The Empire is already hard-pressed and the contest has only been going a short while," the Lord Regent said as they came up to him. He was clearly not a man who indulged in small talk, diving straight into whatever matter he wished to discuss. "This may turn out to be either the shortest Dùbhlan over which we have presided or the most interesting. Regardless, the punters are in for a treat."

"I wouldn't count the Empire out so quickly, Master," Rhiannon replied with good cheer. As she spoke, she moved towards a large holographic tank which was set in the middle of the room, displaying symbols representing Human and Lukratza units along with damage markers. It was providing real-time updates and Danny could see unit symbols winking out in time to the pulses of pain that assailed her shield. There were a few scattered units that clearly didn't align to either of the competing sides; the Mages were in the field, keeping a watchful and neutral eye.

The Lord Regent looked up from the hologram where he had been contemplating the action. His eyes moved across Danny, looking at her for only a second before turning his attention to Rhiannon. She felt a wave of revulsion come across her when they briefly made eye contact but stifled it, unwilling to show that man that he unsettled her. "I am not. I know a little about what humans are capable of, being one of them myself. When it comes to our kind, you should always expect the unexpected."

"Indeed. I know the reputation of this Colonel Brydges and he seems capable. The briefing packets with which we were provided say that he's always looking for innovative ideas from his subordinates and never ignores the possibility of a good one just because of who it comes from. It seems he made a name for himself in that Kingforsaken business at Pollux a few years back but not in a conventional sense. A rescue of one of his squads against direct orders to retreat."

"That sounds like a good person to be leading the fight for the Empire then. I have not been back to the Empire for years yet I cannot help but cheer for its success – in private of course." Danny started and wondered why the man was lying when every person in the room knew that to be untrue.

"Of course, Master. I do the same myself, although I think our opinions are in the minority, especially in the Citadel."

"Hmm." The Lord Regent seemed bored with the comparison of the sides and snapped his gaze back to the hologram. "I am handing out the assignments for the week. We are well prepared for the next three days but I assumed that the Empire would capitulate sooner than that, so I did not bother to work out the rest. Looking at this though, I may have been mistaken."

Rhiannon was taken aback by that statement. It wasn't often the Lord Regent admitted he could make mistakes, instead of acting like everything went according to a plan that only he held in his head. Even weirder, this was the second mistake he had made in recent times. *Perhaps he's losing his grip*, she thought. She was terrified then, thinking that the Lord Regent would have read the thought as she'd had it. She relaxed when she remembered that they all had their mental shields up, negating any risk of mind-reading for the time being. The Lord Regent continued speaking, unaware of the small flash of angst.

"Which brings me to you. You and your... apprentice will be heading out to observe the southernmost section of the Lukratza's front line four days from now. Report anything that could be seen as a violation of the agreement to me immediately. Only to me."

"Yes, Master." Why only to him? She would reserve her judgement until she returned from the assignment. Even so, that wasn't standard operating procedure.

"When you return, come and find me. I have some news from the outer systems that you may find interesting. I do not want to go into too much detail until I get the information verified but initial reports indicate an Imperial ship was destroyed by an unknown agency. This could be what we have been waiting for since the Order was founded."

10

CHAPTER TEN

Reynolds had been in the same position on the ground for so long that his limbs were stiff and he desperately needed to take a leak. Normally, he would go in the power armour he was wearing but he thought it was a little too soon into the contest to start drinking his own recycled urine. There would be time enough for that later, a thought that made him grimace. "Haley, come and take over for me."

Haley sauntered over to him and bent down to take the binoculars out of his hands, a cigarette hanging out of the corner of her mouth – unlit. She swapped with Reynolds who ran over to the nearest tree to relieve himself. Once done, he re-joined his squad who looked, of all things, bored.

It was the morning of the second day of the Dùbhlan and so far, his team hadn't been called upon. They had been nervous about the first day, expecting to be called in to fight fires all over the battlefield but they had been surplus to requirements; Reynolds wasn't sure whether that was a good thing or not. One thing he did know was that in the killing fields in front of him, hundreds of his comrades had died in the mud while he had sat there and watched them. They would have been calling for help or for their mothers, but senior command hadn't seen the need to send support to any one location. Unseen by the rest of his squad, he clenched his fist, only releasing the tension when the armoured gauntlet started to grind in protest.

They had positioned themselves at the top of a hill a klick behind the front lines and settled in, waiting for a distress call that would send them scrambling for the chopper. Their vantage point and the lack of trees gave them an impressive vista of the jungle below yet there were enough shrubs and bushes around them that they wouldn't stand out to anyone looking towards the hill.

The pilot who had been assigned to them for the day was just as bored as they were – he had challenged Sinclair to a game of tic-tac-toe, scratching a board into the dirt. Sinclair had lost seven games in a row and he wasn't best pleased. He'd lost a month's wage to the clever pilot but was convinced that he could win it all back in the next game.

After the initial charge of the Lukratza, things had settled down a bit. Four hundred soldiers had lost their lives on the first day compared to only one hundred and fifty Lukratza. The 1st Royal Earth Division had just about managed to hold the line and the Lukratza had retreated, no doubt to concoct one scheme or another. Reynolds had read numerous intelligence reports on the journey to Midway detailing the Lukratza's normal modus operandi and this just didn't seem like them. They were up to something; he was sure of it. Why else would they try something so out of the ordinary when they were more than capable of simply punching through the lines and taking control of Brydges' CIC?

"Johnson, Baker, report."

"Johnson here. All quiet. Nothing moving between us and the front lines, sir. Didn't you say they were likely to send scouts to infiltrate the base?"

"I did. They normally try and take out the command centre of their opponent as soon as they can, ensuring that their enemy is blind as well as deaf. Head out another two hundred yards and then swing back round to the north. If you don't have any contact, fall in."

"Copy."

"Reynolds to Command Actual."

"Command Actual. Go ahead."

"No contact yet, sir. I'm going to wait another half an hour and then move to another position. How's it going at the front?"

"We're holding. They only seem to be sending out small units, testing the line to see where we're weakest. I've got two regiments playing catch-up, reinforcing each point as it's tested."

"Sir, recommend cancelling those movements. I've got a hunch they're measuring the response times. If they know how many troops are going to reinforce each point and they know how long it will take, it's only a matter of time until they use it as a distraction and hit us somewhere else."

"I'll take it under advisement, Sergeant. Command Actual out."

I should have phrased that better, thought Reynolds. *Doesn't sound like he's going to follow my advice. Why should he, though? He's a Colonel and I'm only a Sergeant. He makes all the important decision – that's why he gets paid the big money.*

His rifle snapped to his shoulder as the shrubbery to his left began to rustle. Dropping to one knee, he aimed at the centre of the movement and motioned with his right hand for Haley and Sinclair to do the same, his finger only momentarily leaving the trigger before snapping back into place.

Although they could see for miles around the hill, the undergrowth in front of them was too thick and dark to penetrate with their eyes alone. He switched to motion sensor in his HUD but quickly blinked it away, the brightly dancing spots of contact causing more confusion than it was worth.

The movement gradually grew more intense and two large bulky figures suddenly burst out of the jungle heading straight for Reynolds. He almost squeezed the trigger but his reflexes allowed him the time to recognise Johnson and Baker springing towards him and he briefly lowered his rifle until they were past. That, and the tags on their armour wouldn't have allowed his rifle to fire at a friendly target anyway.

"Sarge, behind us!" Baker sounded panicked as he ran past.

Johnson and Baker joined the line, spreading themselves out so that they couldn't all be hit with the same explosive at once and thereby effectively eliminating the capabilities of the squad. A silence descended over them as they waited, shattered now and again by faint explosions coming from the front lines.

"Johnson, how many times do I have to tell you to announce you're coming in? And why wasn't anyone watching the motion tracker? You've got them in your heads-up displays for a reason!" Reynolds was furious, forgetting for a second that he himself had tried using the sensor to no avail.

Johnson at least had the good grace to look chastised. "Sorry, sir. It won't happen again. Baker got spooked by movement and took off. I followed him, trying to keep him in my sight. Idiot managed to knock his infrared sensor off his helmet on the way back."

"You're damned right it won't happen again," Reynolds growled, imagining all sorts of punishment that would persuade the men not to repeat their mistake. Another movement in the undergrowth made the team alert again. "This could be it. There shouldn't be any of our guys near us right now so shoot whatever comes out of those trees."

The tension grew ever more palpable as nothing happened and Reynolds wondered if this was another false alarm. With no further warning, a blur shot out of the bush and went straight towards Baker. Two shots rang out, both of them missing their targets as the soldiers quickly noticed that the thing coming towards them was neither nine feet tall nor did it own large, pointy teeth.

Recognising what had bolted towards them, Reynolds burst into laughter. "Found your IR sensor, Baker." The squad couldn't contain their mirth as they stood in a circle around what looked like a small monkey holding a lump of metal in one of its four hands.

Johnson cuffed the back of Bakers helmet. "Idiot."

#

"This is Firebase Gamma! We are under heavy fire and require immediate support!" The gunfire that could be heard in the background of the transmission was accompanied by screams and Reynolds felt glad that they were finally being called upon. Feeling a twinge of guilt at his reaction, he took a second to pinpoint where on the front lines Firebase Gamma was in the map on his HUD. South – fairly close to where they were right now.

"Load up!" he called, then grabbed his Bergen and sprinted for the chopper. He almost beat the pilot, who quickly ran his checks and fired up the engine. Firebase Gamma was only a five-minute ride from their current position, located far to the south of the field; it was only luck that they were close enough to respond in good time.

Once his team was belted into the chopper, it quickly took off and moved at a low altitude towards their target. As far behind the lines as they were, they still couldn't discount attack from an anti-air emplacement so the chopper deployed countermeasures as it went, chaff and flares falling gracefully in its wake like sparks from a huge welder.

The jungle rushed past, the bottom of the chopper only barely scraping by the tops of the palm trees. Reynolds used his HUD to see the current location of the reaction regiments and pinpointed them far to the north, only recently returned from the site of another probe. They weren't going to be any help on this one unless the engagement lasted much longer than Reynolds wanted it to. A quick surge of frustration went through him as he saw that Brydges hadn't taken his advice about the QRF forces on board but he quickly squashed it and deemed it irrelevant to his current circumstances. Still, he was morbidly pleased to be able to say *I told you so* when he next saw the Colonel.

He activated the radio in his armour and went straight through to the operator in the Firebase.

"Firebase Gamma, this is Sergeant Reynolds. We are five minutes out from your position. Give me a sitrep."

"Reynolds, sir! This is Corporal Harfield. We're holding the southern end of the line. The Lukratza started an attack about ten minutes ago. Hundreds of them came streaming out of the jungle along with large beasts that I've never seen before. We were holding them back, diverting them into our firing lines until one of the beasts got to the barricade. It began ripping it apart with its claws and started eating it! Soon as it had done that, the Lukratza came through the gap. We're moving back to the rally point by fireteams hoping that the heavy weapon emplacements will make a difference. Sir, nothing we had could even touch that beast's hide."

News of the Lukratza using new weapons didn't come as a surprise to Reynolds considering the meeting in the conference rooms with Kir'ami. It also wasn't a surprise that the Lukratza were attacking Firebase Gamma – if they broke through the lines there, they could swing up behind the rest of the human troops and catch them between two forces. It would be a disaster and they would be hard-pressed to push them back.

"Have you got any light machine guns?"

"Yes, sir."

"Set them on sentry mode and then double-time back to the rally point. If you've got any mines, lay them out in a random pattern. It might dissuade any Lukratza from following you too quickly. We'll land to the north of you and set up to hit them from the side. Once I give the go command, push back."

"Copy. Firebase Gamma out." The relief in the Corporal's voice at being given a concrete plan of action was palpable.

The base itself was coming into view and Reynolds thought that Corporal Harfield had been overly optimistic. Bullets and laser beams were flying back and forth between the embattled troops and he could make out human soldiers retreating in a relatively orderly fashion. He took note of squads installing light machine guns as quickly as they could, using the buildings for cover. Other squads were setting mines while a few brave men and women were exchanging fire with the advancing Lukratza, buying time for their comrades with their lives.

Their job completed, Reynolds saw the moment they received the order to retreat. Bolting back towards the rally point at top speed, the troops who had previously been holding the lines passed through more troops who had their rifles at the ready. Moving a hundred yards beyond the holding line, they turned and aimed back towards the Lukratza who were visibly confused – they'd been expecting to fight for every inch but suddenly the way forward seemed clear. The troops leapfrogged all the way back to the rally point and set a perimeter, waiting for Reynolds' command to take revenge.

The Lukratza took full advantage of the lull, charging forwards at the first opportunity. The beast that had eaten the barricade had finished its work and was now lumbering towards what Reynolds recognised as the command centre for the Firebase. Rounding the first corners of the pre-fabricated buildings erected on the site, the Lukratza's front rank was mown down without warning. A guttural roar erupted from the attacking troops and they turned their weapons against the light machine guns that had been the cause of the setback. They were demolished in seconds but completed their task of buying as much time as possible for the humans to rally.

Convinced that the human's trickery had been exhausted, the Lukratza moved forward again. They didn't understand humans very well if they thought that would be the only surprise left behind for them.

Taking this opportunity to set his squad in the right place, Reynolds waved at the pilot of the chopper who swooped in to land along the northern periphery of Firebase Gamma, touching dirt only for the time it took for him and his team to bail out and check their corners.

On this side of the Firebase there was no barricade, perhaps hinting at the confidence, even arrogance, the garrison had held regarding their own fighting abilities. There were no clear defences that they could use if they had to retreat and this simple oversight could lead to slaughter if something went wrong – something exactly like this. Reynolds resolved to have a stern word with the Firebase Commander if they both survived the day.

Reynolds brought his wandering mind back to the matter at hand. As the chopper had flown overhead, he had taken note of where the retreating soldiers had placed the mines and so was surprised when the Lukratza soldiers went past them without setting them off. An increasing number of reptilian troops filtered into the wide area between the buildings where the humans had lain yet another trap without causing a single mine to explode. He reached for his radio, about to get in contact with Harfield when all of the mines in the field went off at the same time. He grinned - if nothing else, the shock of having so many explosives go off simultaneously should make the Lukratza think twice.

A loud explosion rent the air and innumerable lizards disappeared, either dismembered or vaporised by the resulting release of energy. A stunned silence fell over the battlefield as the Lukratza took stock of their situation, shaken by the sudden turn of events. Shaking their heads and baring their teeth, they began to advance once more.

11

CHAPTER ELEVEN

The time had come for the counter-attack. "Baker, Haley, you're with me. Johnson, you've got Sinclair. Use the buildings for cover and move as close as you can without compromising your exit. Make the most of your heavy weapons and with any luck, we'll be the difference." All four soldiers nodded at him and set about ensuring they were ready.

Reynolds touched the radio on his shoulder. "Harfield, you there?"

"Yes, sir."

"Your guys ready when I give the signal?"

"Yes, sir." A brief silence came over the comm, and then, "What's the signal?"

"Gunfire, Corporal." Reynolds grinned wickedly in anticipation. Glancing to his right, he saw Johnson and Sinclair moving rapidly between the buildings, positioning themselves along one flank of the attacking Lukratza. He motioned with his left hand towards Baker and Haley who complied with the order, moving further away to his left with their rifles at the ready. Reynolds removed the corner camera attachment from his helmet and clipped it onto his gloves. Shuffling closer to the danger zone, he edged his glove around the side of the building he was using for cover until he could see the Lukratza streaming past in the street beyond in the corner of his HUD. He made damned sure that nothing else was poking around the corner for fear of losing it.

One particularly large and ugly specimen was standing in the middle of the road, directing the other lizards to sweep through the buildings. The Lukratza were in full hunting mode. Gone were the neat formations of soldiers that had assaulted the barricades, replaced with a mob of lizards, all of whom were looking to add as many human scalps to their collection as possible. He wondered if that was something they did – collect human scalps. He decided that they probably just ate their victims, although he couldn't be sure. He didn't want to find out either way.

Reynolds muttered a prayer to the King under his breath and touched his radio once more. "Go."

He darted to the side and went down on one knee in one smooth motion, pulling his gun up until the crosshairs in his vision were aligned perfectly with the largest Lukratza's forehead. He gently squeezed the trigger, allowing a short burst of bullets to escape from the weapon and snap on their way to the target, whistling as they went. Caught out, the Lukratza had barely enough time to register surprise before Reynolds' shots slammed through his brain, instantly dropping the monster to the floor. One down.

The Lukratza surrounding the deceased commander stopped in their tracks and searched for the source of the bullets. Another roar started to build in their combined throats but was cut short as the rest of Reynolds' squad opened fire, the combined fire turning the open area into a killing zone. Lukratza troops started dropping like flies which startled those still left alive, pushing them closer to blind panic. Reynolds switched his aim to another lizard and then to another, his finger only pulling on the trigger in short, sharp bursts, changing targets before he had seen that the previous one had dropped, sure that he wouldn't miss his mark.

They knew where he was now. Return fire started to splash the wall next to him, forcing him to roll across the alley to the next corner. He cursed Kir'ami under his breath, hating the insect for allowing the lizards to use lasers when all they had were conventional bullets.

71

A small drop of sizzling concrete landed on his arm and began to burn his armour, wisps of smoke gently rising past his face as if mocking him. Reynolds took a second to shake the mixture off his arm before it caused any permanent damage and went back to searching for his next targets, leaving a distinct scorch mark on the power armour.

It was harder to find anything to kill now, not because they were running out of enemies but because the light from the Lukratza's laser rifles was flashing in his vision. It was like being in a nightclub but without the benefits of the alcohol.

The Lukratza had noticed that there were only a few soldiers causing the devastation and their ranks swelled in response, preparing for a mass attack. Their attention was so focused on Reynolds' squad that they didn't notice the returning garrison until it was too late.

Streaming up from the southeast, a wave of human soldiers began pouring lead into the flank of the Lukratza force. The collective body of lizards shook, shuddered and then broke, running full pelt back towards no-man's land without a care for their own safety.

"Chase," Reynolds breathlessly ordered before taking his own advice, not giving the garrison time to gather themselves or stop to begin celebrating. The relentless wave of humans forced the Lukratza further and further from the base back towards the barricade, where the lizards filtered through the gaps made by their beasts like a tide going back out to sea. It was hard going on the humans who had to run past and over first the bodies of their victims and then of their own dead. The attacking line began to fragment as those squads who had a clear way forward pulled ahead of their comrades, making a dangerous situation even more precarious.

Bang!

Reynolds found himself on his back looking up at the sky, a beautiful blue, unmarred by the conflict happening on the ground beneath it. For a few terrifying seconds, he lost the ability to speak or tilt his head. Unable to do anything else, he stared at the sky and pleaded with it to open up and

72

swallow him whole, anything to stop the incessant ringing in his ears. Although his prayers weren't answered by a dramatic end to his life, the ringing began to slowly die out in his ears and he became aware of the incessant gunfire still flying over his head.

"Sarge! Sarge! Geoff!" Johnson sounded panicked. "Baker, get him up. Anyone see what happened to him?"

"Glancing hit from a Lukratza laser," Haley replied. "Clipped him on his helmet before it bounced off somewhere else."

Thank the King for the reflective qualities of his helmet.

"Sarge, you okay?" Baker pulled Reynolds up by the arm and dusted his back off, checking the Sergeant's helmet for cracks or penetration. There were none and Baker stood back, waiting for Reynolds to answer his question with his concern clear by the way he stood close, ready to catch him should he fall.

"I'm fine, kid." Despite the bravado, Reynolds certainly didn't feel fine. He was going to have the kingdom's worst headache in the morning and he could feel the contents of his stomach going round and round like a washing machine. He sighed. Again, all the problems with alcohol without the pleasure of actually having to drink it. "What's the situation?"

"They've gone past the barricade," Johnson said. "The beasts are the only things left. I just heard Corporal Harfield order his units to begin repairs and man the wall, but they're refusing to go anywhere near it until those beasts are gone. Problem is, they don't look like they're inclined to move off peacefully."

"Sounds like a job for us," Reynolds said, "so check your ammo and form up." His squad complied. "Let's finish the job so we can all go get some well-earned rest."

A second, stronger wave of nausea rolled over him and he took a second to gather himself. "Can one of you get me some painkillers before we go, though?"

\#

"Bloody hell! That is one big beast," Sinclair whistled. Having hastily swallowed the painkillers that Haley had handed him, Reynolds and his team had made their way to the barricades and now stood staring at the thing still slowly consuming the metal as if were made of butter. It was almost twenty feet tall and they had to strain their necks to look up that high. They wondered what had inspired the Lukratza to make something so monstrous. It was like an ogre from one of those old fairy tales, the kind that only came out at night and did their best to eat the local children.

"Not a problem, right, Sarge?" Johnson said with a grin. Reynolds wondered where he got his confidence from. He knew that it was a challenge to keep his voice level, let alone consider going head-to-head with a monster.

"Not a problem, boys and girls," Reynolds winked at Sinclair with false bravado, his face visible through the plate on the front of his helmet. "Split back into two teams and open fire when I say so. If it runs at you, stop firing and move out of the way. That should stop it focusing on you and start to think about the others."

"State the obvious, Sarge." Baker received another clip around the head for his quip.

After rogering up, they split up and hunkered down behind some smouldering debris left from the initial assault. The Firebase was a mess and Reynolds knew that the garrison would have to put in a lot of hard work to get it back to what it had been before the assault. He was thankful that he wouldn't be asked to help. He might be good at being a soldier but he wasn't necessarily the most practical person in the worlds. He was so much better at bringing things down than he was at raising them.

The garrison themselves were keeping their distance and Reynolds suddenly thought that this would make good entertainment if it were on a television show. Like gladiators preparing to do battle before the masses, his squad were pumping themselves up and waiting for the command to make contact. Baker was even playing to the assembled crowd, stretching and showing off in his own inimitable way. A quick word from Johnson brought him back down to earth.

"Open fire."

Five guns started barking simultaneously, startling the beast so much that it dropped its meal and jumped in a comedic manner. The gathered mass released a small laugh and then, some stumbling awkwardly to the amusement of their peers, scrambled for cover when the beast chucked some debris their way. The good humour was enough to bring a sense of normality to this otherwise strange day.

The debris collided with a wall and splintered into fragments. The beast's aim was so bad that it prompted a member of the garrison to reappear around the corner. He about-faced and dropped his trousers, showing his bare behind to the beast.

"Our weapons really aren't having any effect! Harfield wasn't kidding," Baker shouted over the cacophony.

The soldier who was mooning the beast was yanked back around the corner as if by a shepherd's crook. Reynolds pitied the brave soldier, not doubting that a non-commissioned officer was reaming the poor guy out even as they were still fighting the beast. Hell, that's what he would have done.

"Switch to armour-piercing rounds," Reynolds ordered as he made the change himself. Selecting the icon in his HUD took a matter of seconds, the rifle linked to the power armour following the instructions straight away. The beast shook its head like a horse trying to get rid of five extremely irritating flies. Its head swung round and its gaze focused on Reynolds. As the squad pumped more and more bullets into the beast, still with no effect, it finally decided to get rid of the nuisance.

The ground shook as it charged straight at Reynolds, its momentum building with each thunderous footstep. A wave of fear crept down his spine as the lumbering monstrosity got closer and he was forced into action when the beast rammed its shoulder into the debris that he was using for cover, sending the metal flying at speed. A roll-away at the last second saved his life and he looked desperately around to see where the beast had gone.

A large, scaled fist nearly the size of a civilian vehicle slammed down just next to him and he located it at last. Standing directly above him, the beast cocked its head to the side as if considering how best to squash Reynolds like a bug.

He raised his rifle as the crosshairs in his HUD went haywire, trying to get a clean shot at the beast's head but never managing to get one. The other fist came out of his blind spot and hit his left side, throwing him well over ten metres. He slammed into a wall, thanking the King for the second time in a matter of minutes for the armour he was wearing as it had likely saved his life. That was two hits on his head today alone, probably reducing the overall number of brain cells he had left. The beast followed him, intent on finishing its kill.

Before he could gather his thoughts, the beast had grabbed him and now held him above the ground, his feet dangling in the air as he ineffectually tried to release himself. Reaching behind his back, he plucked his combat knife out of its sheath and plunged it into the fist, to no effect. The pressure on his chest gradually increased as the beast tried to squeeze the life out of him, the once protective armour now a prison that he could not escape from.

Reynolds found it harder and harder to breathe and an ominous black started creeping around the edge of his vision. He had enough presence of mind to hold onto his knife, stabbing again and again at the fist with each resulting thrust getting weaker as he began to lose the battle. Just when he thought that his life was forfeit, the grip lessened and he gulped down a lungful of clean, life-giving air.

The beast released him and he collapsed, his legs not responding to his attempts to make them move. It almost didn't occur to him to wonder why he had been granted a reprieve until he heard a short, sharp whistle followed by a shout. He recognised that voice but right that second, he couldn't place it and neither did he care.

"OI! Beastie! I'm much tastier than he is, he's all stringy where I'm all muscle. I work out much harder than he does! Grubs up, freak, come and get it!" Johnson was doing an odd sort of dance through the clearing, his rifle trained on the monster's head in preparation to fire. He let off a couple of rounds at its head, causing it to flinch a little then zero back in on Johnson. Like the leviathan it was, it slowly began walking towards him, the speed once again rising with each thunderclap of a step.

There was no way that Johnson would be able to escape the beast if it caught hold of him and it was moving far faster than Reynolds had thought possible.

"Johnson, get out of the way before it crushes you!"

"No can do, Sarge. I've got an idea that should work."

"SHOULD?"

With a cheeky wink towards Reynolds and with the beast now charging full pelt towards him, Johnson calmly switched his rifle to the grenade attachment and set his stance. Sighting the gun at the monster, he controlled his breathing and, in a single, smooth pull, fired a grenade right at his target. For a gut-wrenching second, it looked like he had missed but then it connected in a way that Reynolds hadn't been expecting.

The beast swallowed the grenade, a single tooth tumbling to the ground as it was knocked out by the moving lump of metal. It continued its charge and Reynolds thought that Johnson's gambit had failed. He was about to scream at Johnson again to move out of the way when the grenade detonated. The beast toppled, ploughing its face into the ground. Its momentum was so huge that it slid along the floor in the direction it had been travelling, eventually coming to a stop only centimetres from Johnson's boot.

Although he looked pale and sweaty, a huge smile broke out on Johnson's face. He put his foot on top of the beast's head and slung his rifle over his shoulder like a hunter posing with his prize.

"Take a picture for me, Sarge?"

12

CHAPTER TWELVE

As one of the most respected Masters in the Order, Rhiannon had access to the files that told the story of the neophytes embarking on their training at the Citadel. She rarely took advantage of the opportunity, instead, allowing her personal experiences with each student to dictate her impressions of them. This time though, she was too curious about Danny to resist, sensing the raw power that the child contained – even if Danny herself didn't know the full extent of her capabilities.

She was nothing less than a conundrum, a fascination. A child who came from a normal family on Earth, a family with no history of Magick going as far back through their ancestry as the Order could see. It was high time that Rhiannon looked through her files in detail having only given them a glance when Danny was assigned to her. She wondered what she would find as she explored their depths.

Rhiannon had made herself a cup of English Breakfast tea in the cafeteria (her favourite) and grabbed a couple of pastries to nibble on whilst she was doing her research on the child prodigy. She made her way through the maze of the Citadel back to her private room and took a seat at the plain maple desk set against the wall underneath the single window. The Order preached that their members should refrain from collecting pointless possessions – the only thing they needed was the power they controlled. This meant that despite her high status amongst her peers, Rhiannon had a very austere room.

The morning sunlight streamed through the opening and Rhiannon closed her eyes for a second, feeling its warmth on her face. She concentrated on her breathing and settled on a slow and steady rhythm, allowing the low levels of activity around the Citadel to wash through her. She was glad that she had been able to lower her shield even if only for a second, knowing that she would not have dared do so later in the day when the fighting was typically greater. With a sigh, she built the barrier back up, trapped once more in the confined space of her own mind.

Anyone looking around her room may have assumed that she had only recently been assigned to it but the truth was that Rhiannon had slept in that same room, in the same bed since she was a lowly Apprentice. She was pleased that she had no desire for material possessions, preferring to spend most of her time either in contemplation or honing her not inconsiderable skills. The only concession she made to decorations was a vase of beautiful, pink peonies she kept in the sunlight on the desk. She was rather proud of these flowers as she used her own life force to keep them alive and blooming, allowing a trickle of energy to flow out of her body and into the flowers before she went to sleep every night. Those peonies had been on her desk the entire time she had inhabited this room – over sixty years. With luck and planning, she hoped to keep them alive for many years to come; a side effect of the Magick was that users could extend their lifetimes far beyond what was natural for their respective species.

The elderly woman gobbled down the first of the pastries before activating her datapad, finding the files on Danny and then throwing them onto the wall so she could peruse them more easily – her eyesight wasn't what it used to be. She skimmed over the basics, mostly ignoring the information she already knew. Eventually, her eyes were drawn to one titbit of information that was buried in the mass. She leaned forward on her elbows and focused, reading a report from Danny's favourite primary school teacher. As she took it all in, she thought to herself, *why was this child not found sooner? Her potential was on full display years before any of our scouts caught her.*

#

Her primary school teacher, Mrs Barton, had never written a bad word about Danny. By all accounts, she was an intelligent, inquisitive child, not dissimilar to most children her age. For three years the school reports sent home to Danny's parents had said much the same thing – Danny is a kind, caring and bright member of her class. She never caused any problems at school and had a good group of friends. Danny was one of the quieter children, allowing her friends to take the spotlight when the group was noticed at all.

There was a small note that had been filed away by Mrs Barton but never sent to Danny's parents that drew Rhiannon's attention and curiosity. Mrs Barton had written this note but decided not to send it and had recorded her reasons why. It was this that Rhiannon now read.

"Seeing as Danny has never caused any trouble in the past, I have not contacted her parents regarding this matter. It is curious, though. In all my years of teaching, I've never seen anything like this and I wouldn't expect to in the future."

Attached was the initial letter that Mrs Barton had written.

"There was an incident this afternoon. As you know, we have a rabbit that is kept in the classroom so that the children can learn to look after something other than themselves. Unfortunately, it sometimes helps teach the children how to cope with loss as we found this afternoon when we came in from our lunch break to find that the current rabbit, Pepper, had died. The classroom burst out crying and, after covering the animal's hutch with a cloth, I left the room to fetch the caretaker to come and dispose of the body.

When I returned, Danny was holding Pepper in her lap – still clearly dead. She was crying heavily, as was the rest of the class. I asked her to hand the rabbit over to Mr Hanson and she leaned over to give the rabbit

80

one last kiss before doing so. When she moved her head away the rabbit was sat happily in her lap, acting like nothing untoward had happened! It was unharmed and indeed had a huge appetite – it proceeded to devour three whole carrots! I can't explain it; it's like Danny brought it back to life but I can't find a single explanation as to how!"

Rhiannon smiled to herself, satisfied with the results of her research. How indeed?

13

CHAPTER THIRTEEN

Colonel Brydges took a second to compose himself before replying to General Webb's question. Ariel could see that Brydges was tired, even though the holographic representation had leached all colour from his face. He could see it in the set of his face, in the way he held his shoulders.

Tired, yes – but had he cracked already? He didn't think so but with so many lives at stake, he had to be sure.

"Yes, sir, I think we can do it. We've taken moderate to heavy casualties across the board but they haven't broken through the lines as of yet. These first two days we've only been testing each other, seeing where the other is weakest. The Lukratza almost scored a win at the southern end of the line but a timely intervention from Reynolds and his squad kept the area firmly under our control. We've made inroads to the north of the battlefield, taking out at least two Lukratza listening posts. The battalion manning Firebase Gamma was cut in half, however, meaning that we may be needing the reinforcements from the fleet sooner rather than later. I know they're our only ones. I know that we will be using them before we want to. I still think it's our best option at this juncture."

Ariel took a swig of his coffee (hot this time) and had a hard think about whether to send down the reinforcements. It was ultimately his choice but he intended to defer to Brydges' judgement as he was the commander in the field. He had to remember that the Colonel would do things differently from how he himself would do them but Brydges had a good track record of getting things done.

Should they really be committing the remaining division onto the field at this stage, when everything was still up in the air? Doing so would mean that they had everything on the table, so to speak, and if they suffered another catastrophe like the one at Firebase Gamma, they would have no backup plan. The doubts were almost unbearable and would only get harder as the contest wore on, sat on the sidelines as he was.

"Colonel, what is your plan going forward? I refuse to send those troops down to the planet if all you're thinking of doing is sitting tight and waiting for something to happen. Persuade me."

A flash of irritation went across Brydges' face, noticed by the General but controlled quickly. "I plan to take a leaf out of the Lukratza's book, sir. A common strategy of theirs is to use shock troops and penetrate lines quickly, taking the opposing commander out of the fight and claiming a quick victory. I've been thinking, why not do the same to them?"

Why not indeed? A bold idea, definitive action. Ariel finished his coffee whilst John explained his thinking and outlined exactly what he intended to do. Getting to the bottom of the mug, he instantly signalled to Davies that he wanted it refilled. Davies came forward, took the mug and moved off to get another. That man really was a brilliant aide.

Making the most of the distraction that Davies had provided, he took a few minutes to think through Brydges' plan from every angle, only looking back towards the hologram when Davies had returned and placed a fresh mug in his hands. John had finished talking and was waiting patiently for an assessment of his plans. He knew that trying to push the General for a response was never going to get results.

"My apologies. You know I can't function without caffeine. Go on."

John added the finishing details as General Webb took his first sip of the new coffee.

"I want to pull as many troops from the line tomorrow evening and marshal them at the north end of the battlefield, about a kilometre back.

We will set up as many automated weapons as we can to give the appearance that we're still there, leaving only a minimal garrison at each point. We would be relying on our special forces to keep us safe throughout the night with routine patrols through and around the lines – with one exception. Reynolds and his squad would spend the night getting as close to the Lukratza commander as they can, laying traps and sending back information to make the assault as easy as possible. Then – simple. Spear through their lines to their command centre and win the Dùbhlan."

"Simple? Why would I send you reinforcements when you sound about as experienced as a child playing one of these ridiculous war simulations they call games?" Ariel was furious and allowed the anger to creep into his voice. "I've always thought highly of you, John, but I don't like the way you're talking right now."

"Respectfully, sir, I was only trying to sound confident. I have no illusions about how difficult this could be – but please, this could be our only chance to win before time and attrition prove to be the reason for our defeat! We can't lose, sir, not with the King watching our every move. We have to pull through." Webb heard the undertone of fear in the Colonel's voice and tried his best to ignore it.

"Come on, John. You must understand how difficult this is for me – I have no control over what happens and can only send you more good men and women to be killed. They put their faith in us not to waste their lives needlessly – they want to think that there is always a good reason for the sacrifice. Why are you confident you can pull this off?"

John seemed taken aback by the General's apologetic and reasoned tone, perhaps never thinking that he would back down so easily. *Ariel has always been different,* John thought. *He seems to genuinely care for the troops under his command and wants to do right by them. Something that we have in common. I hope to remain as empathetic as the General at the end of the Dùbhlan.*

"I am confident because I know that the men and women we have here are the best the Empire has to offer. I'm confident because I know that with veterans like Reynolds, we can outthink the Lukratza, even if we can't beat them toe to toe. I'm *confident*, sir", he stressed the last confident, "because I know that you wouldn't have given me command if you didn't think I could do it."

"Damn right I wouldn't have, son." Ariel smiled at John, feeling for himself the confidence that John was displaying. "All right. You can have the reinforcements. But if it doesn't feel right to you – or to Reynolds – I want you to rethink the plan and come up with a way to win that doesn't include more people dying."

"Thank you, sir." John saluted and took his leave, cutting the transmission off. Alone with his thoughts, Ariel sat for a long time with visions of the disaster at Pollux racing through his mind.

#

Emerging from the conference room situated off to the side of the main thoroughfare and back onto the brightly illuminated bridge, Ariel's first thought was that everyone was busier and much more stressed than when he had left them. Officers were running between different stations whilst Admiral Leystrom stood in his usual position in front of the projector, looking for all the worlds like a conductor in front of his orchestra. Despite the flurry of activity around him, Leystrom seemed calm and collected, not allowing any inner turmoil, if he had any, to show on his face. He was always professional and that was something that Ariel appreciated about the Admiral. It was easy to have a good working relationship with the man.

"What's the word, Admiral?" Ariel asked as he stood next to him, clasping his hands behind his back and nodding at the puzzled sailors.

"General. I hope your conference was productive?"

"It was, it was. Don't dodge the question, George."

"You know me too well, I fear. We've been getting transient contacts around the edge of the Midway system but they disappear before we can get more than a generalised fix on their location. Considering that all traffic in and out of the system is meant to be curtailed during the Dùbhlan, I'm concerned that it could be pirates trying to get a look in whilst we are focused on what's happening on the ground."

"Anything I can do?" "Thank you for the offer but no, there isn't. You know you'd be useless anyway." A smile lifted the corner of the Admiral's face.

Ariel clutched at his heart, feigning injury at the words from Leystrom. "Oh, you wound me! I suppose I'll have to go back to my office and eat more custard creams while I wait for the navy's finest like yourself to decide what to do. Let me know if you want any, by the way. Custard creams, I mean. There aren't many left." He patted his slowly expanding waistline to emphasise his point.

Leystrom grinned at him, knowing that his words were meant in jest. "You're a cantankerous old git, aren't you? Go on, shoo! Off my bridge."

"Yes, sir! No, sir! Three bags full, sir!" Ariel sketched a mock salute and turned to leave the bridge with a sense of satisfaction. Sometimes it was good to have a little banter, even with a squid like Leystrom. The Admiral covered his eyes until the General was well on his way to leaving the room.

Just before the hatch closed behind him, he heard Leystrom order, "Ladies and Gentlemen. I don't want to bother the rest of the fleet with something like this so, with that in mind, Helmsman, set a course for the outer belt. Tell Captain Jones that he's in command until our return."

14

CHAPTER FOURTEEN

Having requested reinforcements from General Webb and received permission from Kir'ami to deploy them to the field, the final division of royal troops disembarked the fleet above and began their descent to Midway. There was no way that the humans could hide the movement from the Lukratza as they would have been informed by the Kir'archi that had filed the paperwork. On top of that, the simple lack of anything in the deep black made it ridiculously easy for ship sensors to see that smallest speck of dust on the far side of the system. They knew they were coming and they knew that meant an attack. This would give them time to prepare but that was something that couldn't be avoided.

Despite this, John Brydges thought that the incoming troops were a positive thing. Sure, their arrival signalled to the human forces that things were worse than high command were willing to admit but it meant that the contest was being taken seriously. It was being supported by the King so they should take pride in their actions and do them to the best of their ability. These additional troops would ensure that they were able to do so.

A huge number of dropships swooped down into the newly deforested landing areas only a couple of kilometres behind the front lines. The troops, who could see what was happening, began cheering when the birds came into sight, buoyed by the sight of reinforcements. The shouts of joy and happiness continued right until the troops began filtering out of the ships, forming up into squares in the parade ground to the front of the landing area. They looked up at the blue sky, squinting at the bright light after weeks cooped up on carriers and cruisers and grinned at each other. They may be on their way to death and glory but damn, it was a fine day.

#

Colonel Brydges had resorted to an old-fashioned paper map, in the end, preferring the feel of pushing counters representing his forces across the table to the distant, hollow feel of interacting with the holographic unit. With a sense of satisfaction, he added the counters for the 5th Royal Division to the map, clustering them together on the open space they had cleared especially for their arrival. He was waiting for Sergeant Reynolds, whom he had summoned from the front lines in order to give him his new mission in person. What an important and decisive mission it could prove to be.

While he waited, he received updates from his command staff on the status of the new troops, signed provision orders and gave orders to Captains and Lieutenants kilometres away to put this risky plan into action. He reached for his mug and smiled, silently thanking General Webb for the generous gift he had sent down on the last supply ship – coffee beans from Ariel's personal stock. It was nice to be appreciated. He hoped that he would live up to the General's high expectations.

A knock sounded from the direction of the tent door and he turned and waved Reynolds into the hub. "You made it, Sergeant," he said and pointed at a padded chair that had been added around the edge of the map. "Take a seat."

"Thank you, sir." Reynolds took his time getting comfortable but was eventually ready. "You wanted to see me?"

"I did. I'm sure you've heard the latest news?"

"Yes, sir. Another full division sent down with the compliments of the General. He must really like you. Let's hope that they haven't gone rusty after so long watching the rest of us look heroic on the big screen. I take it this means something big is coming?"

Brydges took another swig of his coffee and had a sudden thought. "Sergeant, would you like some coffee?"

"That's very kind, sir, but I would prefer tea if you have any."

The Colonel did and asked his aide to fetch some for the Sergeant. "Something big is absolutely happening, Geoff. We're gonna turn the tables on the Lukratza and do to them the thing that they're so famous for – cut their heads off and win."

"Very good, sir. I presume that you summoning me here from greener pastures means that you have a particular role in mind for me and the kids." Reynolds accepted a cup of tea from the aide and wrapped his hands around it, blowing softly over the top to cool it down. "What'll it be?"

"Cut straight to the heart of it, Geoff! That's one of the reasons I like you."

"With the other being my devilishly good looks?"

Brydges burst into laughter. "By the King, I needed that. Haven't laughed for days. I don't think I've ever heard anything as preposterous as what you've just said!"

Reynolds took a second to look hurt before joining the Colonel in laughter. "Come on, sir, tell me what you want me to do."

John stood up and began pacing around the map. Looking down at the floor, Reynolds noticed that although this tent had only been erected for a few days, the Colonel had already worn track marks around the table. He had known that Brydges had been worried (and who wouldn't be, stuck in such an important yet stressful position as this), but he hadn't thought the contest had gotten to him as much as it clearly had.

"Okay. Here's how it is. It is my belief that the longer this battle continues, the more likely it will be that we will be defeated, and defeated soundly. We need to take decisive action and we need to take it now whilst we still have the soldiers and the wherewithal to make a difference." He slammed his fist onto the table to punctuate his point. The force of the blow knocked over two of the counters representing the new troops and

John had the presence of mind to look sheepish whilst picking them up and putting them back in their proper place.

It's a good thing I don't believe in omens, Reynolds thought, *else that would have been one of the more obvious signs I'd ever been sent.*

The Colonel continued with his explanation, not noticing the reticence that had crossed Reynolds' face.

"A swift assault will be launched by all available human forces tomorrow morning, heading for where we think the Lukratza command post is located," he said as he pointed at the marker for the Lukratza commander. "I want you and your *kids* to head off tonight, infiltrate their lines and prepare some surprises for them. Your ultimate objective is the command post. I want you to confirm that the commander is indeed where we think he is and report back to me as soon as you know. By the time you get there, the entirety of the Lukratza forces should be in an uproar, making your job a little harder. We will move as quickly as we can and I expect that we will be only a few minutes from your location when you radio through with the confirmation. I know that contacting us like that will give your position away but we should be close enough that you haven't got to survive long on your own."

John paused for breath and Reynolds took advantage of the break to interject. "Do I have permission to attack in a rearwards direction back towards headquarters if the heat on us is too much?"

John smiled at the terminology the Sergeant had used. The typical British soldier was too proud to ever use the word *retreat* and John was one of the most prideful soldiers that he had ever met.

"You do. I want you alive, Geoff. You're no good to anyone if you're dead."

"Thank you, sir."

"Don't mention it. Do you understand your orders and will you carry them out to the best of your ability?" The sudden formality signalled an end to the briefing and high time that Reynolds returned to the field.

"Yes, sir." Reynolds stood to attention and saluted the Colonel. The salute was returned crisply and promptly and Brydges was once again proud to be commanding men like Reynolds.

"Go make hell, Geoff. Gear up and commence the mission as soon as you're able. I'll see you tomorrow and I'll make sure you get a good spot next to me so the cameras can recognise the reason we won and show it to the entire galaxy."

15

CHAPTER FIFTEEN

Danny fell back in her chair, exhausted from the effort of keeping the heavy metal weight floating in front of her. Sweat coursed down her face and back as she opened her mouth, desperately trying to pull in some sweet, fresh and much-needed air. Somehow, she had thought that using Magick to move objects would be easier than the physical exertion it would have required yet it seemed to make no difference between using her mind and using her hands.

She reached up without thinking to move a stray lock of blonde hair that had attached itself to her forehead and looked over at Rhiannon, trying to gauge how well she had done. Although in Danny's limited experience her master was not normally one to show emotion outwardly without good reason, she noticed a smile on Rhiannon's face and felt her spirits lift.

"Good, little one. That was the best yet." Rhiannon walked in front of Danny and put her hands on her hips. She pursed her lips in thought and seemed to be reluctant to speak her next thoughts, an inner conflict raging within that was entirely new to the woman. Eventually, she said, "how much have you been practising the shielding technique I demonstrated to you?"

"I've been practising as my free time allows, Master. I think I have it down. Not sure that it's to the sort of level that you expect though – or even to a level that I'd like. I'm sorry that I haven't been able to devote as much time to it as I think you would have preferred." Danny looked abashed and was genuinely upset that she hadn't been able to work as hard as was expected.

"We know that you can do it, child, as you so definitively proved when the Dùbhlan commenced. The question is, can you do it when someone is actively trying to get through your defences? It's a completely different proposition, much harder by far. Whether it's the mind of an opponent or a physical object that is being used to target you, it is possible to defend yourself."

This was new – Danny hadn't really thought through the implications of her telepathy and the thought of someone intentionally trying to get into her mind made her shudder with apprehension. Thinking about it, she realised that it was only part and parcel of the deal. There would always be someone willing to hurt her and the better prepared she was for any such attempt, the more likely it would be that she would survive – even come out on top.

"The next activity will involve some risk to yourself, child. I'm going to direct some objects towards your body at speed and I want you to do what you think is best to ensure your own safety." This time, the older woman didn't miss the flash of fear that went across her apprentice's face.

Rhiannon moved away from Danny and went to stand next to a spindly-looking wooden table that had been placed at the far wall of the practice room they had booked for that evening's work. Arrayed on the table were sharp, scary-looking spikes of various sizes and materials, fanned out as if a merchant were selling his wares on the high street of a time long gone. Some were barely longer than her little finger and others were taller than she.

Danny especially didn't like the look of the longest ones, spikes that were almost three metres in length and made from the finest Damascus steel. They all had sharp points, some of which she knew would be barely thicker than a single atom. Danny wasn't looking forward to her Master firing them at her. What if she missed one? She could be seriously injured, possibly even killed. Her breathing shortened once more.

"I'm going to give you a second to compose yourself and put your shield in place", Rhiannon said, "before commencing the test. We'll start with the smaller ones and work our way up. I want you to deflect the missiles, rather than stop them cold. Can you remember why?"

"Because deflecting a missile uses less power and allows me to conserve energy for a later time." Danny was a quick student as she kept proving time after time. She always had been and she seemed to vacuum up knowledge like she was starved of it.

"Good. How you actually achieve the deflection is up to you. I will give you no more hints about the theory. However, I would appreciate it if you directed the missiles to the side of the room – if you send one back towards me, there'll be trouble!" The smile on Rhiannon's face took the sting out of the harsh tone she had used.

Danny grinned back at her, her nervousness building and making her adrenaline kick in. "Of course, Master." She felt her heart pounding against her chest and a faint sheen of sweat broke out once again on her forehead which had only just dried from her previous exertions.

Rhiannon nodded encouragingly at Danny and then stood as still as she possibly could, gathering her own power and allowing Danny to concentrate.

Danny reached inwards and found that little nub of power in her mind, the one that she was becoming ever more familiar with. It had continued talking to her over the last few days, its voice becoming stronger and more insistent the longer that she practised with Rhiannon. The Magick reached back to her like a long-lost friend, its relief at being acknowledged palpable. Danny almost lost her concentration when she felt pure hunger rushing to envelop her, overpowering her own emotions and nearly forcing her down into the black pit from which it had come.

She pushed with all her might yet remained still as a statue, the inner battle taking all of her resources and willpower just to remain on equal footing with the Magick. A minor sense of victory coursed through her as she gained ground, increasing the mental pressure until she broke through the nub and felt the power surge through her body like electricity. It was under her control for the moment, her strength of character commanding the Magick to do her bidding.

Focusing now on the happy memories of her family that had been so effective in shielding her the first time, she proceeded to build a wall. She knew she had been successful when the background chatter of other people's thoughts stopped completely and she realised that this was the first time she had truly been alone since she had arrived on Midway. Alone that was, except for the crystal clarity of The Voice.

So far, so good. The next step in the process was to expand the wall beyond her body. It only had to be a couple of inches but that may as well have been on a whole other planet. The sheer focus that was required to build the shield was daunting and Danny began to sweat more freely, thrust into this activity having barely recovered from her previous exertions – although that may have been the point. In the future, who (if any) of her opponents would allow her to rest before attacking?

Distantly, she heard the authoritative yet reassuring voice of Master Rhiannon breaking her own previous statement about providing no extra help.

"Think of an elastic band, child. Don't force the shield away from your body, stretch it!"

Danny complied. She slowly began to stretch the shield away from herself, first a toe and then a foot. Her leg followed and as she stretched the shield away from her other leg, the whole thing snapped into place. She opened her eyes.

She lifted her arm up to shoulder level and could just about see a dim haze surrounding it, like the heat rising from an open fire. She raised her other arm to check and then looked down at her legs – all hazy! She smiled with satisfaction.

Rhiannon looked at her appraisingly. No apprentice had ever mastered this technique so quickly or so seemingly effortlessly. "Danny, I'm going to throw one of the spikes at you – not yet telekinetically but with my hands. Are you prepared?"

Danny nodded sharply, not wanting to break her concentration, then took a deep, steadying breath. Grasping the smallest spike in her right hand, Rhiannon took a half step forward and launched the spike like a projectile directly at Danny's chest, point first.

The one thing that Danny hadn't been expecting was for time to take a break. As soon as the spike left her Master's hand, the world around her went into slow motion. She had all the time in the worlds to think about where she wanted to send the spike and even more time to think, really think about how hard she wanted to do so. The spike got ever closer and when it was only a few inches away from the shield she had placed around her body, Danny reached out with her hand and gently nudged the spike onto a new course, barely taking any momentum off the throw.

As she finished nudging, time crept back up to full speed and the metal zinged towards the wall, exactly where Danny had wanted it to go. It hit with a thud and a shower of sparks and then stayed stuck in place, vibrating ever so slightly from the force of its impact. The vibrations slowly eased and then stopped. Danny beamed as she realised that she had passed the first test.

"Perfect. Are you now ready for the full test?" Rhiannon asked, a small note of wonder creeping into her voice. Danny nodded. "If you think your shield is about to fail, nod your head once and I will end the attempt."

Rhiannon motioned with her arm and used her Magick to lift all the remaining spikes on the table into the air at once. They began an odd dance around her head, swirling around Rhiannon like an orrery with the Master taking the place of the star. *I hope she's prepared for this.*

The next test began. The spikes moved quickly towards her head yet, once again, time slowed for Danny. She felt overwhelmed with glee as she realised that this was something she could do, something she was good

96

at! Barely registering each projectile, Danny redirected each and every one of them towards the wall with minimal effort, noticing, through the field of metal, the look on her Master's face. What had started as a concerned look slowly changed to a look of amazement and Danny giggled at the sheer ridiculousness of the situation.

As the last projectile was sent on its merry way to its final destination, time snapped back to normal and Danny turned to look at the results of her handiwork. "How did I do, Master?" She spoke the words sweetly, already knowing the answer.

Rhiannon glared at Danny for a second, the look of amazement still evident on her face before turning to look at the wall where Danny had sent the metal spikes. Staring back at her was a smiling face made from the projectiles. She made a faint spluttering noise and then looked back at Danny, utterly speechless.

16

CHAPTER SIXTEEN

Hanging majestically above Midway, the Royal fleet looked for all the worlds like a school of sharks on the hunt for something tasty in one of old Earth's beautiful oceans. Ships of all sizes were on display, announcing to the Midway System that they were there with full regalia on their hulls. This fleet was put together to make an impression and had been pooled from the various combat fleets operating throughout human space. Smaller destroyers and corvettes wove in between the larger cruisers and battleships in a stunning display of confidence and control. All ships were oriented to protect the vulnerable carriers who regularly birthed patrols of fighter ships, often swelling the numbers of craft inhabiting this one small portion of space.

Captain Jones was now in temporary command of the fleet as the Admiral had gone hunting at the edge of the system, taking the H.M.S *Excellence* with him. Captain Jones was known amongst the sailors as a good commanding officer, even if he was a bit of a stickler for the rules. Not a bad reputation to have although he was far from universally liked. It wasn't the job of an officer in the navy to be popular but this small fact irritated him a little.

Luckily for him, the job he had been handed was simple. He was to maintain station, keeping an eye on both the battle taking place on the planet and also on the Lukratza fleet that was currently patrolling the far side of Midway. *Easy,* he thought, *all I need to do is keep the troops supplied with copious amounts of food and ammunition and the rest should take care of itself.* Had the situation remained the same, it would indeed have been simple. Things were about to take a turn for the worse and there was nothing that any human in the fleet could have done about it, nor was it to be something that they could have seen coming.

The anomalies that had lured Admiral Leystrom away from the planet hadn't been idle in the intervening period. Five huge, pitch-black ships had been slowly creeping closer to Midway, undetected by even the most advanced sensors of either the Empire or the Hegemony. The ships had corrected their courses incrementally as the hours and days had passed until each one was pointed directly at the five largest ships in the Royal Fleet. They planned on reducing the number of living beings in the system substantially and to begin, they were going to take down the largest threats first before moving on to the other, less important ships.

As Captain Jones sat down with his first cup of tea for the day (ship time) the spectres increased their speed, going twice and then three times as fast as they had been in only seconds. Quickly, they were well past the point where the Royal ship's sensors should have sounded an alarm for a potential collision. As they came closer, an observer may have noticed (had they been in a position to notice them at all) that their shapes began to change, with each streamlining down into a bullet head, speeding towards their targets.

The alarms brazenly began to rouse the crews but it was too late – the spectral projectiles punched through the hulls of the Royal ships like they were made of paper. Captain Jones had only just lifted the cup to his mouth for a first sip when he was unceremoniously dragged into space through a rather large gap in the bulkhead. Flashes of light showed him where the escaping gases from the ships briefly caught fire before winking out in the oxygen-depleted vacuum. At this point, Captain Jones only had fifteen seconds before he lost consciousness.

In the first five seconds, he noticed a stream of small black ships coming around from their initial punch and arcing back towards his ship.

It split even further, going from one arm that moved with purpose down to smaller rivers before crushing back through the warship and speeding off to their next target. He wondered where they had come from but would never discover the answer.

In the next five seconds, Captain Jones looked around at his fleet. Of the two hundred warships the humans had brought with them, fully three-quarters of them were in pieces. The few remaining intact ships had begun to light their main engines, but Captain Jones thought that they had little chance of escaping this unknown enemy. *It's quite beautiful*, he thought to himself, *all the different colours. Almost like fireworks. What have the Lukratza done?* He wasn't sure it was the Lukratza though, as he had never heard of them deploying a weapon like this before. Who else could it possibly be?

In the last five seconds, the remaining human ships were wiped from existence. So many lives lost in such little time. The debris from the ships and the bodies of the sailors were caught in Midway's gravity, destined to burn up in the atmosphere in a newly made meteor shower. The black ships pulled themselves back together and began their short journey on to the planet of Midway itself. The soldiers down there had no way of knowing what was happening and wouldn't until their daily check-in. Captain Jones had to warn them! But how?

A darkness had been creeping in around the edge of his vision and now it took over completely. *This is why I'm not a morning person.*

17

CHAPTER SEVENTEEN

What the recruiting Sergeant never told you throughout his song and dance, of course, was how fabulous and rewarding the life of a soldier would prove to be. *If I ever find the son of a bitch who conned me into signing up, I'm gonna wipe the damned smile off his face,* Sergeant Reynolds thought as he fought his way through the thick undergrowth in the dark towards the Lukratza command centre. He slapped at his neck as he received yet another bite from one of the innumerable pests that seemed to inhabit this King-forsaken place. He thought that wearing power armour would have protected him from the nasties that were attacking him but these things were tiny enough to get through any gap in the metal plating. They were making travelling a misery and he was looking forward to getting back onto one of those lovely, air-conditioned and bug-free ships up in orbit when this was all over.

Reynolds and his squad had been marching flat out for seven hours now, having set out on their mission just as the sun had set over Midway on day three of the Dùbhlan. It had been easy going at first, the no-man's land that separated the two sides having been almost completely flattened over the last few days so each had a good view of what the other was doing. That was the most nerve-wracking section of the journey so far, concerned at every moment that the Lukratza would spot them and send some lasers their way. Through a combination of luck and hard-earned skill, they had moved through the area without incident, although they had been bracing for incoming fire the entire time. Even for the veterans like Reynolds and Johnson, it had not been a pleasant experience and was certainly one that none of them would like to repeat.

They'd spent a few hours planting traps, landmines and tripwires galore, making sure to electronically mark them so that any human troops following them up would see them on their HUD. There was no limit to human creativity and they were sure that the Lukratza would miss most of the traps, even if they managed to find and disarm some of them.

At some point in the journey, Johnson had opened a private channel to Reynolds and said, "Sir, did you see that?"

"See what, Johnson? A bit of detail wouldn't hurt."

"Bursts of light in the sky right around where our fleet should be patrolling. It was quick; lots of little flashes like someone trying to talk in Morse code. I've been wracking my brains but I can't come up with a single explanation that isn't bad for us. Either that or I need to go and get reassessed on my Morse code."

"No, I didn't see them. Too focused on not walking into a tree. What were you doing star-gazing anyway?" Reynolds' voice held a tone of mock menace, forcing a small laugh out of his Corporal who knew that he was joking.

"Oh, you know me, Sarge. Always wanting to move onto better and brighter things."

"You're a funny man, Johnson. The squad jester, even. Don't mention anything to the kids yet unless they say something first. I want them to concentrate on what we're doing, rather than something that we can't do anything about. I'll try getting in touch with the Colonel and find out what's happening but I'll have to do it discreetly."

"Copy". Johnson continued moving through the jungle, seemingly mollified and leaving the rest of the squad completely clueless to the conversation the two of them had just held.

Reynolds quickly checked his HUD to make sure that his team were where they were supposed to be before attempting an audio connection (encrypted) back to headquarters.

"Reynolds to Command Actual, do you copy?" A crackling static was his only answer. He tried again. "Reynolds to Command Actual, over."

No reply. That was unusual. He shrugged his shoulders and thought to himself, *must be the jungle. Too much interference.* Reynolds and his squad continued their mission and he resolved to keep trying every fifteen minutes until he received an answer. There had to be someone on the other end of the radio. He tried to ignore the sinking feeling in his gut.

#

Danny had never felt such a volatile mix of emotions all at once. She was excited about going onto the battlefield as an observer but she was also terrified about getting hurt. She was interested to see the Lukratza up-close yet was also concerned about the human fatalities that she had heard about on the news reports, in the overly cheerful voices and huge musical scores that sports reporters loved to use. When she realised that she'd only thought of the human cost of the contest, she also felt guilty. It was no surprise that she felt a little nauseous, with all those feelings swirling around her body, not to mention the mixing pot of hormones teenagers typically had.

The volatile, emotional mix forced the Magickal shield she was maintaining to slip momentarily, allowing a small burst of distant pain to assault her. She reached up to her head and rubbed her temples, willing the shield back into place before silently berating herself. She was becoming more adept at the skill with each passing hour and hadn't allowed herself an incident like this for a while.

Master Rhiannon looked at her out of the corner of her eye having caught the full range of emotions from Danny and thought to herself, *that's a special one. It's not many people who would think of the enemy and feel concern, let alone many children.*

"Are you all packed?" Rhiannon asked cheerfully, trying to distract the young girl. Danny nodded back. "Good. Let's get moving then, shall we?"

It was almost a crime to be awake this early in the morning, Danny thought bitterly. It was still dark outside, with none of the various birds singing in the trees yet. She had never seen the Citadel at this time of day, usually waking up to brilliant sunlight, a comfortable bed and best of all, warmth.

When everyone sensible was still asleep, the two Mages had woken and prepared themselves for their journey out onto the battlefield. Although they were only hoping to be gone for the day, they had packed as many survival essentials as they could into the rucksack that Danny was thrilled to be carrying. Still, there were worse things she could be doing and worse people she could be doing it with. She checked herself as she noticed that this was the happiest she had been since her abduction, as well as the first time in a long time she hadn't been missing her family. Her feeling of guilt increased exponentially.

Without a further word to each other, the two women, one a Mage and the other an aspirant, crept through the Citadel careful not to cause any unnecessary noise. Making their way down to the hangar towards the bottom of the immense castle, they passed the dormitories of the Apprentices and the private bedrooms of the Masters and more promising pupils.

The only life present in the rooms they went through were the Apprentices who had drawn the short straw of making the Citadel presentable for the coming day. None of them made eye contact with the two trespassers, keeping their heads down and staying focused on their tasks of either sweeping the floor or wiping the walls with a small cloth. Their passage through the working Apprentices would normally have been the most interesting thing to happen to the youngsters all day.

After walking through eerie rooms for a few minutes, they came to a gravity lift that would let them essentially fall all the way to the bottom of the Citadel to the hangar. Without pausing for thought, they stepped into the slightly purple light and dropped, coming out at the bottom of the lift shaft into the cavernous space of the main hangar. Nothing more than a sheltered cave at the bottom of the plateau on which the Citadel rested, the hangar was a hive of activity even at this time of day.

A nexus for all movement in and out of the Citadel, the hangar was permanently crewed by mechanics who were servicing the vehicles that would be taking today's quota of Masters and their Apprentices down to the jungle below. None of them wanted to be the reason a vehicle failed and potentially caused harm to one of the powerful Mages. Their lives wouldn't be worth living if that happened and they knew it. They were fearful of the Lord Regent who ruled the Order by making examples of those unfortunate enough to displease him. In the past, those examples had been terrifying enough to act as a very effective deterrent.

The Order had been run in various ways by previous Lord Regents. Some would take control and install a council, relying on the combined wisdom of many Masters to guide the Order forward. Others would become dictators and lay down the law, not allowing anyone to step out of line. Punishments under these leaders could be as mundane as pulling extra chores. There were the rare examples of people who made such a big mistake that they were given corporal punishment with the most extreme one being death. The incumbent Lord Regent was the least popular one to hold the post for centuries. No one dared to inform him of that fact, however, rightfully fearing the consequences.

"Wait here," Rhiannon ordered and marched off to see the Hangar Controller to be assigned a vehicle. Danny complied, gratefully taking the heavy rucksack off her already aching back and finding a quiet corner to sit in. The walls of the hangar were surprisingly dry. Danny had expected them to be damp like so many other subterranean spaces and she put her weight on the bare rock, relieved at the cold touch of the material. She was pleasantly surprised when she realised that although the rock was cold, it certainly wasn't wet. Rhiannon was looking for the Controller long enough that Danny began to doze off, half-dreaming about what she expected to see on the battlefield.

#

In her vibrantly coloured dream, she was running through the jungle at full speed underneath a bruised and ethereal sky, a feeling of terror weighing her down and the instruction of *don't look back* reverberating through her brain. Trees and shrubs were exploding on either side of her and she narrowly missed tripping over a root that had suddenly appeared right in front of her. Stumbling, she recovered her balance and ran off at full pelt. She felt someone pursuing her and tried to run faster to stay ahead of them, understanding without knowing why that they were gaining on her. It was a losing proposition and, as the minutes went by, the feeling of intense terror grew stronger and more consuming.

A palm tree crashed down to the earth in front of her and she tried vaulting over it, clearing the tree by some margin only to lose her footing on the other side. She collapsed onto the floor, her ankle throbbing with a dull pain. She thought that she had sprained it at the very least but couldn't be sure, begging someone, anyone, to come and help her. Looking back the way she had come, her face went ashen as she saw what had been chasing her.

It wasn't what she had expected in the slightest. She had assumed that she was being chased by one of the huge reptilian Lukratza but all she could see was a black shadow looming in the undergrowth behind her. Now that she had stopped moving, so too had the shadow and it floated menacingly on the spot, neither moving closer nor making any sound that Danny could hear. The minutes stretched as neither of them moved, only staring at each other – one with malevolence, the other with fear. How long they stayed like that Danny couldn't tell but there grew in the background a thumping noise as if something huge and heavy were walking her way.

The noise got louder and louder until it drowned out all other sounds. The trees were shaking in their anchorage in the dirt and Danny thought that she could see them parting where the thing making the cacophony was coming her way. It came closer and Danny was sure that she was going to die, the trees right in front of her moving to the side to allow something through…

#

She was snapped out of her reverie when a couple of mechanics sauntered past gossiping excitedly between themselves and otherwise unaware of their surroundings. Blinking quickly to allow her eyes time to adjust to the low lighting, an intense feeling of relief came over her as she realised that the thumping noise in her dream had only been the mechanics walking towards her. She must have subliminally incorporated it into the dream and was glad that it was something as mundane as the technicians. Her heart was going nineteen to the dozen in her chest and she focused on her breathing, slowly bringing herself back to normal.

Despite her parents having taught her that eavesdropping was the height of bad manners, she couldn't help but listen to the workers, desperate as she was to know more about how the Empire was faring in the contest. She justified it to herself by saying that she wasn't spying – as an Apprentice, she was only collecting intelligence that would help her get through the day. That justification assuaged the slight feeling of guilt.

"I can't see the Empire lasting longer than a couple more days. The Lukratza have them on the ropes at the moment. I shouldn't have put my money on the Empire to win but I'm a romantic at heart."

"You should never put money on anything, Kevin. You never win when you gamble. Besides, word through the grapevine is that Colonel Brydges is pushing for something big. They got reinforcements yesterday, remember?"

"Yeah, mate, you're right." The technicians were getting further away from Danny. "Hey, you know what else I heard? The Royal Fleet has gone dark; no one has heard anything from them for hours. I wonder if they're bending the rules a bit, maybe trying to help Brydges a bit more overtly."

"Maybe. Wouldn't like to be the King if that's the case, though. I heard the Hegemon threatened them with all-out war if they broke the status quo."

"No! You can't be serious! That would break all the rules, even the ones that they don't tell anyone else about!" Their voices faded as they moved away, intent on going about their day.

Danny started as Rhiannon reappeared in front of her. Rhiannon was throwing a set of keys up and down in her hand, seemingly not noticing the state that Danny had worked herself into. "Got us a ride. Ready?"

As the two of them got settled in the air taxi, Danny couldn't stop thinking about what she had overheard…

#

Admiral Leystrom was less than pleased. The anomalies that they had been chasing in the outer system had turned out to be nothing. There were no ships, stations or satellites this far out towards the heliosphere that would explain what his sensors had been telling him. It had taken them a day to get out here and it would take them another day to get back and it was all now looking like time wasted.

"Comms, get me a link back to Captain Jones."

"Yes, sir."

Leystrom cast his eye over the holographic representation of the battlefield on Midway while he waited for the link to be established. Curiously, he noticed that the time stamp showing the last update was from the day before which he was sure was wrong as updates should have been pushed through from the main fleet hourly. Communication with the planet, even with planets elsewhere in the Milky Way, was instantaneous and there shouldn't have been a delay in connecting. He frowned and looked back up at his staff.

"Someone figure out why my display is out of date. This is the flagship, for King's sake! This should be a tightly run affair, no room for mistakes!" The crew knew that when the Admiral was in this mood, it was best to keep their heads down and get on with the job, lest they upset him any further.

A nervous technician bent down to begin looking into the problem but stopped when Comms shouted across the room to the Admiral, "Sir, I can't establish communication back to Midway. All I get is static as if someone is jamming the link. I've attempted the connection three times already, as well as trying the emergency channels. There's no one listening, sir."

Leystrom's stomach sank without him really understanding why. He couldn't explain the feeling, only understood that his gut was telling him something was wrong – and his gut had never made a mistake in the past.

"Keep trying. The second you hear from Captain Jones, you put him right through to me. In the meantime, Helm, get us back to Midway at best speed. Push the engines past the red line as much as you can without blowing up my ship."

The crew acknowledged his latest orders and went about their tasks. Seconds later, the Admiral was gently bracing himself against the dais in front of him as the huge engines of the *Excellence* swung the ship around onto a new heading and pushed the behemoth back towards Midway.

What in the worlds was going on?

18

CHAPTER EIGHTEEN

It was time for the final operation to commence. Colonel Brydges felt not a small amount of pride as he once more thought through the details of his plan, not least because it was an audacious undertaking. Hit the enemy where they are least expecting it; not a new idea but perhaps something that the Lukratza weren't fully prepared for. A decidedly underappreciated human trait, that – when cornered, fight for your lives. His troops had worked through the night to make sure that they were prepared for the coming engagement by getting into position, ensuring they had enough ammo and checking and double-checking that their supply lines would be good enough to keep up with the main bulk of the army. Once that was all completed, they had hunkered down to attempt to get some sleep before the big push, trying to be as fresh as possible for the coming day.

The only kink in the plan was that local comms seemed to be down. Brydges came up with a solution to that particular problem by using runners but it could become a major problem later on down the line as his troops became spread out and out of sight of each other. He swore to himself that when they'd won, he would find out who was responsible and make them pay for adding to his problems.

The final section reported readiness and Brydges clapped his hands together once, then motioned his aides to come and join him. The early morning light filtered through the trees and he thought that it made the jungle rather beautiful. The air was cool and felt fresh with a small breeze blowing through the area. A perfect moment to begin his march to victory. He took a deep breath and mentally prepared himself for the big push.

"Report to the Division Commanders and let them know that they can begin operations ten minutes from now. Report back to me with their confirmations."

The aides moved off at a run and he soon lost sight of them in the mass of men. Brydges stood calmly and waited for them to come back. This was it. The late night and the rushing around had all led to this one moment. By this time tomorrow, it would be over and they would be victorious, he was sure. It was unimaginable that they would fail.

One at a time, the aides came back, each out of breath and each reporting that the Commanders had copied and understood. Satisfied that everything was in order, Brydges smiled once more, eager to get underway. They waited for the few remaining minutes to tick slowly off the clock until, at long last, the moment had arrived.

In unison, thirty thousand men and women began marching towards the Lukratza without any fanfare, slowly filtering into the jungle, beginning in fire teams and then in whole battalions. Colonel Brydges waited for most of them to disappear into the shrubs before heading off himself, his bodyguard unit keeping a watchful eye on both him and their surroundings, rifles at the ready.

Cry havoc and let slip the dogs of war, he thought to himself. He thought that he was a very learned man and had spent a huge amount of time in his younger years reading through the classics, Shakespeare and Sun Tzu among them. Speaking of dogs of war, he wondered what Sergeant Reynolds was doing at this very moment. He hadn't heard from him all night which was unusual for someone as professional as the Sergeant.

#

Sergeant Reynolds was once again lying down on the job. He was actually struggling to stay awake at that moment having been on the move through the entire night. They had made it to the Lukratza command centre and confirmed that the commander was present at the site by tapping into the covered landlines that permeated the area. Although they hadn't seen the commander in person, they had been able to determine his rough location by the number of heavily encrypted messages going to and from the building slightly to the north of the compound. They couldn't read the contents of the messages themselves but the sheer volume of data being sent was enough for Reynolds to make the call that he was there.

They'd had persistent communication problems all night, meaning that they had not been able to report back to headquarters as they should have done. As with the traps that they had encountered previously, they electronically tagged the building so any of their comrades who made it this far would know exactly where to go. The Lukratza shouldn't be able to read the tags – the only thing the guys in procurement thought could read the tags was a human set of armour, suitably geared up with the relevant software. Only time would tell.

The main mission should have begun by now. Reynolds' squad was getting increasingly bored, waiting for orders to either attack the commander's compound or attack in a rearwards direction back towards the main force. Not usually one to second guess himself, Reynolds was having a hard time making a choice. There had been no distant gunfire on a scale large enough to make him believe the Colonel's force was nearby and there hadn't been an exploitable opportunity in the Lukratza guards' routine to make him think an assault on their own would work. He didn't want to get caught in a hopeless situation without knowing that there was support nearby and that there was no evidence that it was.

"What are we waiting for, Sarge?" Baker was whining. He was standing guard at the rear of the squad, making sure that nothing crept up on them from behind. They were on a small hill just outside the compound, the adaptive surface of their armour allowing them to hide in the greenery without being noticed. Reynolds had wondered why the Lukratza hadn't posted a guard on this hill considering it had such a great view of their base. He had decided that they were so confident about keeping the humans far away from this point that they didn't feel a need to.

"We are waiting to see if an opportunity presents itself," Reynolds replied. "Stop kicking that rock around and pay attention to what's in front of you!" This was what he imagined having actual children was like. Thank the King he had never had any - his squad were hard work enough.

"Sorry, Sarge," Baker sounded suitably contrite.

Johnson came up beside Reynolds, touching him gently on the shoulder. On a private channel, he said, "He's right, sir. We've been here for hours. If you want my recommendation, we should head back towards the main force as soon as we can; that communication problem is making me nervous."

Reynolds thought about his reply. Johnson was correct to offer his opinion like that and Reynolds was pleased that he hadn't done so over the general channel. They still hadn't informed the rest of the team about the communications blackout and he didn't intend to – there was nothing that any of them could do about it, at least until they got their gear back to the workshop. There was no point worrying them about something beyond their control.

He nodded once at Johnson in reply and he seemed to get the intent, Johnson turned around and went across to Haley who was laid on her front, scanning the compound intently and slapped her on the back. She flashed him an "Okay" signal with her hands but kept her eyes trained firmly on the compound ahead, taking in as much intelligence as she could. What she didn't manage to remember would be recorded by the armour's systems and a team of spooks would analyse it later.

"Right, load up. We're gonna head back to the Colonel and tell him what we've seen."

"We're not gonna attack, sir?" Sinclair sounded like he was disappointed they wouldn't be running kamikaze-style into the Lukratza base.

"No, Sinclair, we're not. They haven't given us any decent openings and I've become quite fond of you all."

Baker sniggered over the comms and then realised that he was broadcasting to the whole team. "Sorry, sir. It's just, we think you're alright as well." Good recovery.

"You're an ass, Baker," Haley commented sweetly.

Baker flipped her the bird and looked back at Reynolds. "Want me to take point, Sarge?"

"Yeah. Sinclair, you're rear guard. Let's get back home, boys and girls. I'm sure the Colonel has the kettle on for us already."

#

It's funny how easy it was for your mind to start wandering, especially when you were moving through terrain you'd already recently been through. This sort of inattention was dangerous and could sometimes be lethal, as Baker was almost to find out.

The march back was boring. All they had to do was move at a decent speed and stay ready for something unexpected. As they went, they double-checked all the traps that they had marked, ensuring that they were blatantly obvious to the grunts heading in the opposite direction. Some of the traps had either been removed, repositioned or had the electronics tags removed by a particularly eagle-eyed Lukratza. They made sure to double-tag any new traps they found.

Perhaps the fact that nothing untoward had happened to them made them lazy on the way back. Perhaps it was how long they had been active without taking any stimulants. Or perhaps it was the fact that the jungle was so thick in places that it made the motion of trackers almost impossible to use. Regardless, none of them were prepared for the patrol of Lukratza that came storming out of the jungle from their right.

The runners were in their midst before the squad had time to react. A particularly ugly specimen collided with Baker way out in front, knocking him down to the ground. There were six of them and they were causing havoc without any warning. Luckily, Reynolds, Johnson and Haley were awake enough to realise what was happening and they opened fire on the lizards, being careful not to point the barrels of their rifles in Baker's direction as much as possible.

Reynolds' first shot was a lucky one and it took the head clean off one of the smaller reptiles before Haley took the legs from under another. Johnson eschewed the use of his rifle in such close quarters, drew his combat knife and moved in to engage the lizards. The wicked blade glinted in the sunlight as he charged, confident enough in his close combat ability to go toe to toe with a biological war machine over nine feet tall.

Baker was awake enough to mentally recover from the shock of the collision, moving quickly to both turn his fall into a roll and draw his knife in one smooth motion. He turned, now with a low centre of gravity and thrust the knife at the Lukratza who had hit him and who was now shaking his head from side to side as if trying to get rid of cobwebs. The knife slid into the reptile's shoulder, going through the natural armour without trouble and causing a terrifying roar of pain that sent birds fluttering from the treetops nearby.

The Lukratza kicked Baker in the chest, sending him flying eight feet through the air. The knife was caught in its shoulder but it didn't seem to slow down the behemoth. It chased him and, turning its head slightly to the side with its teeth bared, went for Baker's neck. Baker raised an arm, an instinctive reaction that saved his life. Instead of connecting with his neck, the reptile wrapped its jaws around his arm and then simply bit.

Baker screamed. He was now widely, rudely and completely awake. The pitch and volume of his scream gave the Lukratza pause for thought and it shook its head again, still bothered by the imaginary cobwebs. Taking one last look at Baker as if regretful that it wouldn't be eating him that day, it bolted off into the undergrowth in the same direction that

Reynolds' squad was travelling, followed at pace by the only other surviving Lukratza.

Baker was in an incredible amount of pain. Reynolds knew this because instead of continuing to scream his head off, Baker had gone deadly silent, staring down at his left hand and forearm – which lay two feet away from him on the blood-splattered grass. Reynolds used his command-level override to silently order Baker's armour suit to inject him with painkillers and a blood-clotting agent, then shouted, "Haley, go help him. Johnson, take Sinclair and sweep through the trees ahead; make sure those buggers aren't waiting to get us again when we head off."

He heard Haley over the channel, "Baker, you're alright! The armour's gonna take the edge off for you. You're okay!" She spent a few minutes checking the rest of him over and making sure he was stable before walking over to Reynolds. "Sarge, he's gonna be fine eventually. I can't see any damage to the rest of his armour other than an almighty crack across his chest plate."

"Good. What can we do about his arm?"

"If we get him back to headquarters in the next three hours or so, the armour should be able to keep the nerve endings in his arm in a good enough condition that they might be able to reattach it. Failing that, they may be able to attach a prosthetic. I've heard they're really lifelike now and knowing Baker, he'd probably get a really flashy one." She smiled weakly, clearly shaken by their close encounter.

"Okay. Keep an eye on him until the others get back." Reynolds waited for Haley to signal an affirmative and then wandered over to the corpses of the four Lukratza who had met their fate at the squad's hands (hand?) that morning.

He gave them a once over but then did a double-take. Kneeling down to the ground, he got a closer look at the lizard's faces. He realised that this was the first time he had truly seen one of them up close (at least, when one of them wasn't trying to kill him) yet he thought something wasn't quite right about them. Their faces weren't matching up to what he thought they should. He noticed the difference and swore.

The Lukratzas' faces were cracked and desiccated, even more than their scaly skin should be. There was a thick, black and viscous liquid oozing from their eyes, streaming down their faces and causing what looked like black lightning marks to spread out wherever they touched it, cracking and corrupting the lizard.

Johnson and Sinclair came crashing back through the trees, shaking their heads to inform Reynolds that the Lukratza had well and truly scarpered. Reynolds waved Johnson over and tapped his helmet right over his ear, indicating that he wanted to switch to a private channel.

"Take a look at these ugly mugs, Johnson. Tell me if you think anything is off."

Johnson went over to the bodies and knelt down, getting closer to the corpses than Reynolds had dared. He swore without realising that Reynolds had done the same, recognising the same things that Reynolds had and then dared to go even further – he reached out and touched the black ooze with his finger, incredibly carefully. Very bad idea.

The black ooze seemed to reach out and grasp at him as he got closer, looking for all the worlds as if it had jumped onto his armour. Johnson shouted and began leaping up and down like a madman. Common sense eventually kicked in and he calmly reached down and wiped the ooze onto the grass. Reluctantly, the ooze let go of Johnson and began creeping back towards the Lukratza bodies.

"What the fuck was that?" Johnson sounded horrified.

"No idea. Never seen anything like it before. Leave it be. It looks like it has a mind of its own and we don't want to be responsible for letting whatever is it loose amongst our boys and girls. Looks like something out of a bad horror movie, one of those old ones that everyone seems to love these days."

Johnson moved away from the bodies and glanced at Baker who was slumped over on the grass, staring blankly at the empty space where his arm should have been. "He gonna be alright, Sarge?"

"If we get him back quickly, he will. Did you notice anything about the Lukratzas' behaviour that struck you as odd?"

After thinking about it for a few seconds, Johnson nodded. "Yeah. They seemed like they were running from something, something from back in the direction of their headquarters. I've never heard of a Lukratza running away from anything before though. I thought that their culture had a taboo about retreating."

"Agreed. Either we've missed the main force going past us or something new is happening. It's now more important than ever that we get back to headquarters, if only for Baker's sake. Five minutes to gather yourself, then we're off."

What Reynolds hadn't said was, *I need to let Brydges know about this. Whatever the Lukratza were running from could be a potential ally for the Empire. That, or a new enemy that's got it in for us all. What in the worlds were they running from?*

19

CHAPTER NINETEEN

Despite being worryingly up close, Danny thought the Lukratza were rather impressive. Majestic, even. Sure, they were bigger versions of the lizards that they had back in the zoos on Earth, but there was something about the way they carried themselves and the way they interacted with each other that led her to believe they had been misrepresented in Earth's media. They were easy to demonise and Danny could see why. From her observations, they were a proud and empathetic race, sure of what they wanted and how to get it – nearly as far from their reputation as was possible.

Rhiannon and Danny had landed at a crudely made airfield just behind the Lukratzas' southern lines after being checked over multiple times by their air traffic controller. Danny could understand the reasoning even at her young age. Anyone could have been in the air taxi – even some royal troops – so they had to make sure that they were who they said they were. This had meant that Rhiannon and Danny had actually been boots on the ground an hour and a half after they originally had planned to be, which was an annoying yet not insurmountable delay.

When they landed, they were ushered directly into a nondescript tent that had been set up to the side of the field, ostensibly for the on-site commander. There they were left alone, both women looking about them with interest at the furniture placed around the spartan space. The Lukratza had something that looked like a chair, although they had a cut-out along the back which Danny assumed was for their tails. The problem was, they were huge compared to any chair that she had seen before. She tried sitting in one but quickly changed her mind when she noticed that her feet were dangling in the air, unable to touch the ground. She felt like a toy in a child's dollhouse and didn't want to embarrass her Master or herself when the commander arrived. She silently giggled to herself as the words from the old nursery rhyme *this chair's too big, this chair's too small* went through her mind.

As she stood back up, the tent flap was briskly peeled back and an average-sized Lukratza came marching into the tent, barely glancing at the two humans as he took a seat behind the huge desk that Danny was sure had only been put there for their benefit. Without any preamble or pleasantries, the Lukratza began talking to them.

"You are Master Rhiannon. We were notified that you would be attending the site today. I stand ready and willing to answer any of your questions and I have allocated a pair of guides to take you around our encampment." The Lukratza leaned back in his chair after making that statement as if daring them to talk. He blinked once, slowly, and Danny noticed that his membranes moved sideways into his eye, not at all the same way as a human.

"Thank you, commander," Rhiannon replied. "I have only one question to ask you before we commence the tour and it is one that I am mandated to ask – and one that you are obligated to answer truthfully. Do you have any chemical or advanced weaponry in your possession and do you intend to use them?"

Danny was taken aback at the sudden change in Rhiannon's demeanour and how different her mentor sounded. Gone was the kind, caring woman who had comforted her when soldiers were dying on the battlefield and in its place was a woman of steel, a woman to be respected. She noticed that her Master had not asked the Lukratza commander for a name and resolved to ask her the reasoning behind that decision the next time they had some privacy.

The Lukratza commander took a second to consider his answer, a newfound respect for the Mage showing in his mien. "Of course we do. Of course we intend to use them."

He stood up, now towering over the two humans. Danny felt like the child she was next to this behemoth of a being.

"You knew this coming in so I fail to understand the question. We have been given permission by the Hegemon himself to win this contest by any and all means possible. That includes, but is not limited to, chemical and advanced weaponry. We have also had some fun employing some of our lesser-known beasts. Take the Lukrog, for example. It made short work of the human's pathetic barricade directly across no-being's land from us two days back. It is the first time we have used this new asset in the field and so far, it has not disappointed." He finished his sentence and remained standing, his insanely large teeth bared viciously in a challenge to Rhiannon. He was almost hoping that she would get angry in return, perhaps looking for a fight.

Rhiannon crossed her arms and planted her feet. Despite the swirl of emotions that was threatening to overpower her at that time, she was calm and collected enough to realise that by exploding at the commander she would be playing directly into his hands – or claws. It was nothing personal - it was all about politics. She hated politics with a passion.

Yes, she had known all of this before even setting foot outside of the Citadel. The rules and regulations that the Mages were sworn to follow had made her ask the question, even though she already knew that she wouldn't like the answer. She was conflicted between the orders that the Lord Regent had given her and her sense of common decency, of fair play. The British Empire had been set up to lose and woe betide them if they managed to come out of the Dùbhlan looking good. It was almost impossible for them to win. Yet there was always hope…

"The Order thanks you for complying. I understand that you have been given… special permissions from the Hegemon. If you have nothing further to add, we would like a quick tour of your compound now."

Rhiannon bowed to punctuate the end of her sentence and then turned on her heels, walking swiftly away from the commander before she could say anything that would get her in trouble. Danny was surprised by the sudden movement from her Master but scrambled to follow, leaving the tent only a few seconds after Rhiannon. The last thing she wanted right then was to be left alone with the commander. She quickly caught up with her Master and fell into step.

"That didn't go well, did it?" Danny inquired, hugely understating how she thought the meeting had gone.

"No, child. The Lukratza are always so infuriating to talk to, consistently acting like we are beneath their notice. Sometimes I feel the only reason that we are allowed to preside over the Dùbhlan is because the Hegemon has told them to put up with us. Still, I should have been better prepared for this meeting – after all, this is hardly the first Lukratza I've spoken to or even the first Dùbhlan I've officiated."

Danny was silent, slightly humbled by the respect her Master was showing by being completely open with her. Before she had a chance to think of a reply, Rhiannon had raised her hand towards two smaller and paler looking Lukratza who were clearly lower down the food chain. Once she had their attention, she said, "I presume you two are the guides that the commander has allocated to us. Take us once around the facility and then we will see what else there is to inspect."

The two lizards glanced sideways at each other and then moved off as if they had been whipped. Rhiannon was not a person to cross and these two looked like they were used to being ordered around. It made sense for the commander to assign two lower-ranked soldiers to look after them, even though good manners would have seen him escort the two women himself. Politics, indeed.

#

The Lukratza compound looked remarkably similar to a human military base. Surrounded by metal barricades with firing steps, there were bland modular buildings set up throughout the centre of the area. The construction of the barricades looked a little sturdier than the human's work, which only made sense when you remembered that the Lukratza weighed almost three times as much as an average human, even one in battle armour. The other thing that Danny noticed was that, although similar in design to human fortifications, the sheer size of the constructs was awe-inspiring.

There were only two exceptions to the rule – the tent in which the two Mages had met the commander and a large cage that was surrounded by nervous Lukratza guards. Rhiannon decided that the cage would be their final stop on the tour. She was a firm believer in leaving the best for last. She was curious about what was inside the cage but didn't want to look overeager lest it be taken for weakness. She wondered if it were the Lukrog that the commander had mentioned so gleefully. She had seen the unreported footage of the assault on Firebase Gamma due to her status as a Master and was intrigued about seeing one of the beasts up close. It didn't occur to her that they could be a threat, even to a Mage of her standing – her faith in her own abilities was too strong for even fleeting self-doubt.

They turned and walked in the opposite direction to the two Lukratza guides who eventually noticed that their charges weren't following them and scrambled to catch up. Rhiannon hoped that Danny had understood her reasoning for doing this and she was satisfied when Danny said, "That was clever. You took control out of their hands and made them follow you, right?"

"Correct. If I have to play politics, I'm going to do it to the best of my ability. You would do well to take all of this on board, even if you choose to go down another route in the future."

Danny nodded her understanding and Rhiannon was pleased that she was able to understand the various machinations and power plays that were being employed. In the short time that she had been mentoring the child, she had proven to be an intelligent and inquisitive learner.

They were escorted around the busy base and they took note of the large number of laser weapons being carried by the troops. Each and every soldier on the barricade was cradling one which was bad news for any attacking humans as the lizards looked like they knew how to use them.

As the tour progressed, they circled around the airfield which dominated the middle of the area. Multiple airships of different designs were resting in the open space, nearly hiding the burns left behind by the fire that had created the field. Rhiannon sighed. The Dùbhlan always caused devastation to the otherwise beautiful planet, something that tore at her every year. The planet would slowly forget, repairing itself and its inhabitants over the course of the next year only to be ravaged once more.

The Lukratza had demolished the greenery in the base with reckless abandon. Rhiannon knew that this was because they were so accustomed to fighting in the Dùbhlan, they understood that any damage they made to the environment would have been repaired in the intervening period before the next one. The jungle was a fast grower, quick to forgive the torment that the combined races of the Hegemony put it through on an annual basis.

They were given a small amount of privacy on the inspection and Danny took advantage of the opportunity to ask her Master the question that had been burning in her brain since they had been in the tent.

"Master, why haven't any of the Lukratza given us their names?"

"In the Lukratza society, giving names is a sign of respect. Other than their hatch mates, a Lukratza could go their entire lives without giving their name to someone. By not giving us their names, they are showing their contempt both of us personally and of the Order. If a Lukratza ever gives you their name, you should feel honoured – it means they think highly enough of you to trust you with such personal information."

Danny lapsed back into a thoughtful silence. She decided there and then that one of her goals in life would be to gain enough respect from a Lukratza to get their name.

Sensing Danny's thoughts, Rhiannon said, "Good luck to you, child. Never, in the entire history of the Order, has a Mage been granted that privilege."

Eventually, Rhiannon decided that they had seen enough of the uniformity of the base. The Order being asked to oversee this particular Dùbhlan was a farce, with the Lukratza able to bend the rules so far that there was almost no point in them being there. She was still intrigued by the cage though, so motioned towards it and demanded that they be shown what was inside.

"You will not want what is in there to be let loose, honoured Master," one of the Lukratza guides said in response, a wicked smile tugging at the corner of his lips as he struggled to pronounce the heavily accented words. At least these lackeys were outwardly showing her the respect she was due even if they were sneering internally. "We will allow you to look in from the outside but no more than that."

The warning from the guides was in such stark contrast to their earlier willingness to help that Rhiannon was taken aback. Realising that their warning meant that whatever was in the cage was incredibly dangerous even to the Lukratza, she motioned an affirmative with her hands and followed the guides over to the cage.

The cage itself had metal plating along the bottom and had a series of steps leading up to a walkway which was thirty feet above ground. When they reached the vicinity of the cage, one of the guides took a bored-looking guard aside and said a few words to him, the contents of the animated discussion remaining unheard by the Mages. Eventually, the guard nodded to the guide and signalled for his troops to move away from the cage, allowing the women access. Danny noted that they didn't move too far away from the cage and her stomach churned as she noticed some of the guards grip their weapons tightly.

They were unable to see what was inside from their present location so they breathlessly ascended the metal steps, deeply interested in what they would find. As they ascended, their view of the base increased to the point where they could see each of the walls over the top of the buildings. Once near the summit, they began to be able to see the ground on the far side, the brush and trees decimated here to provide clear firing lanes. It made Danny feel a deep sadness to see the indiscriminate devastation.

At the top of the staircase, the two women stopped in their tracks. What they were looking at was not what they had expected. Although the commander had made mention of the Lukrog, he hadn't explained what the beast looked like. Having seen the footage from two days earlier, Rhiannon wasn't too surprised by what she saw. Danny had heard rumours of the beast that had attacked the barricade at Firebase Gamma but the news reports hadn't been allowed to show any footage of the attack. If this was the creature in question (and she suspected it was), it was monstrous. She had never seen anything like it in her lifetime and likely never would again.

There were three of them in the cage. Two were bearing scars that made them look even more menacing. The third was larger than the others and coloured in a richer, darker shade that gave the beast a powerful, deadly look; this was clearly the alpha of the pack.

"These are the Lukrog your commander made me aware of?" Rhiannon asked in horror, her emotions flashing through her carefully controlled façade. Despite this, she was intensely fascinated with the beasts and wanted to know all there was to know about them.

"Yes, honoured Master."

"How do you control them?"

"As soon as they are decanted from the birthing vat, they are bonded with a Lukratza beast master. As they grow up, the beast master is constantly there, rewarding them when they do desirable things and punishing them when they do something that is counterproductive."

"What would happen if they turned on your troops?"

"We have a fail-safe installed in their heads, a small demolition charge right next to their brain's control centre which can be activated by the commander on the field at any time. We have never had a Lukrog go rogue, though. They fear the beast masters too much."

Inwardly appalled at the prospect of these creatures existing and anguished about the constant state of pain and fear they must live in, Rhiannon was, once again, outwardly the face of calm and clearly back in control.

One of the smaller Lukrog, a bit more aware of its surroundings than the others, spotted the small human figures at the top of the cage and thundered across the ground towards them. It threw its arms at the side of the cage and roared at the group, allowing a wave of putrid breath to wash over them. Danny stifled a scream and stepped back, yet Rhiannon was unmoved. She, at least, trusted the cage designers.

Rhiannon wiped a string of spittle from her cheek and raised an eyebrow at the Lukratza guide. The guide bared his teeth at her in an approximation of a grin.

"You look like a tasty meal to them, honoured Master. They're conditioned to attack and destroy anything smaller than a Lukratza."

20

CHAPTER TWENTY

They couldn't leave the area around the cage quickly enough after their close encounter with the Lukrog and Rhiannon decided that their next move was to accompany a Lukratza patrol on their route. She had noticed as the tour had progressed that the Lukratza were becoming increasingly agitated and the emotions spilling from the commander would have made her younger self blush. She decided it was best to get Danny away from the base in case it was about to be attacked by the humans, which was how they found themselves deep in the jungle surrounded on all sides by giant lizards. Despite being from different races, Rhiannon knew that being with a group of Lukratza was one of the safest places they could be.

Danny wasn't adept enough yet with her skills to know any better and was enjoying herself. Where she had grown up on Earth, there wasn't a large amount of greenery left – a result of the nuclear war that had given rise to the new British Empire. Taking a hike through all of this life was a new experience for her and she was making the most of it, asking one of the smaller, younger Lukratza a series of questions which, to a human parent, would have been incredibly annoying. Rhiannon made a bet with herself about how long the Lukratza would put up with the questions, thinking that it would only be a matter of time before he got frustrated with the small human. She was pleasantly surprised to be proven wrong.

"How do you keep your teeth so shiny? Do you have any family back home? Which planet do you come from? Are you going to grow any taller? What rank are you? What do you think of the humans? What is THAT?"

The Lukratza was being very patient with her but had begun to look very flustered under the barrage of questions. When she squealed the last question, his head snapped in the direction she was pointing and his laser rifle went to the ready position at his shoulder. He saw what "it" was and lowered the gun again, returning to a relaxed state and giving out an amused chortle. A small monkey-like creature had been staring at them from the branch of a tree but scampered off at the Lukratza's sudden movement.

"It is one of the many infernal pests that litter this planet, little one. It is nothing to worry about," he reassured her. "If you see another like it, please do not make that noise again. Although we are behind the lines, the humans may attack us at any moment. Unless you wish to see me vaporise such a small and cute creature, do not surprise me like that." Although his words were slightly harsh, his tone was warm.

Danny was suitable abashed at startling the Lukratza. Walking ahead of her, Rhiannon allowed herself a smile at the paternal instinct of this one particular lizard. It was nice to make the acquaintance of a Lukratza that didn't appear to be made from the same mould as the others – although, as they said, appearances could be deceptive.

They continued on the patrol for an hour, the jungle coming to life as the sun continued to rise over another glorious day on Midway. Unseen birds began singing and Danny saw small lizards and more of the monkey-like creatures scampering through the trees, following the group as if curious about their intentions. She wondered if the smaller lizards were distant relations of the Lukratza and laughed out loud, drawing a curious look from her new friend.

The walk through the undergrowth was relaxing yet so monotonous that it took Danny a few minutes to realise that the area had gone deadly silent and there was no more movement to be seen. Before she could stop herself, she bumped into Rhiannon's back – her Master had stopped in her tracks as had the rest of the patrol. She strained to see around Rhiannon, wondering what had caused them to stop. At the head of the patrol, the Lukratza who had been walking point had come back to the unit commander and was engaged in an intense discussion, the strong feelings of which Danny could discern even this far away.

Rhiannon told Danny to wait where she was and then stalked over to the two Lukratza and joined the discussion, the Lukratza who had been on point becoming ever more agitated. Suddenly, Rhiannon turned on her heels and sprinted back to the main group, gesturing for Danny to come and join her. Danny ran, concerned by the change in her Master's appearance.

"They've found something up ahead that's really upset them. Stay with your new friend; he's being ordered to make sure you stay safe. I'm going to go forward with the others and investigate. Under no circumstances are you to follow me, do you understand?"

A sudden panic gripped Danny. "Yes, Master."

"This is important, Danny. When I say under no circumstances, I mean it. Say it – do you understand?"

"I understand, Master."

What could possibly have had such an impact on the Lukratza, let alone her Master? The majority of the group, Rhiannon included, moved off into the jungle and she smiled nervously at her friend, thankful that there was someone there to keep her safe.

#

Ten minutes went by without any word from the forward group. Her Lukratza friend had taken to standing underneath a nearby tree, scanning the surrounding area in sections. The colour of his scales made him blend in as if he were wearing a natural camouflage and Danny had to look hard at him to see where he was. If she looked away for too long, it was difficult to pinpoint him again, even though she knew exactly where he was standing.

Danny had sat down on the ground and was throwing sticks and twigs that she had found around her towards a conveniently placed rock, trying to nudge the wood onto new trajectories with her Magick and make a picture. She was so distracted and flustered that it wasn't going well. The image of the Citadel that she was trying to make had degenerated into an unruly mess, perhaps only slightly recognisable if she held her head at the right angle. She sighed and squinted. Perhaps not.

The waiting was unbearable. Without knowing exactly what it was that was happening ahead, she found herself imagining the worst things that could happen. What if they had found a dead patrol, killed by humans? What if it was some dead humans, canny enough to penetrate this far behind enemy lines before their luck ran out? There was just no way to tell and she was torturing herself by going through progressively worse scenarios in her head. As the minutes ticked by without an answer, she decided that she was going to go and have a look.

She stood up and approached her Lukratza friend. "Excuse me?"

He looked at her. "Yes, little one?"

"Don't you think that it's unfair for us to be waiting here? What if they need my help?"

"Your help? You are but a child. What could you possibly offer that one of the most respected Mages in the Order could not?" The words were harsh but Danny understood that the Lukratza didn't intend to be mean – he was just as worried as she was, no doubt.

The question that he had asked in return was a good one and made her think. Danny did a mental inventory of everything that she could offer before settling on one that she thought would have the best chance of persuading the Lukratza to take her to the rest of the patrol. She crossed her fingers and made her choice.

"I know I'm young but I've been told that I have a way of looking at things that wouldn't occur to other people. Besides, how else am I going to learn to be like Master Rhiannon if I never have a chance to challenge myself?"

Although they weren't the most compelling arguments, the Lukratza was clearly bored as well and was worried about his comrades to boot. He was young and naïve and had an overinflated sense of his own importance. He hadn't heard anything over the radio since they left and so decided that whatever situation was developing, his presence could only be a help.

That Danny had been the one to voice her concern also made him feel ashamed, the worst possible feeling that a member of his species could experience. Each Lukratza soldier was trained to be proactive and aggressive, almost to a fault; waiting here seemed to be the furthest thing from it.

"You make some good arguments," he lied to cover his relief, "and coming as they are from a powerful Mage such as yourself, I have been swayed. Stay close to me and do not stray from my side."

Together they followed the others.

#

The path that had been taken by the rest of the patrol was clearly visible to the Lukratza. His keen eyes allowed him to take note of the broken leaves and twigs along with the barely discernible tracks left by the heavier members of the squad. This allowed them to follow swiftly and they made good time, both of them alert to any possible surprises. They had been walking for a fair amount of time before they spotted a clearing ahead and they slowed down, stealthily settling into hiding places in the bushes. The Lukratza motioned for Danny to wait where she was and she complied, allowing the lizard to creep forward for a better look. Not taking her eyes off him this time, she had a clear view of his progress all the way into the open space.

He stopped close to the edge of the clearing and settled on his haunches behind a tree trunk to scan the area. The first thing he saw were the bodies of his patrol. Their faces looked wrong, covered in a black substance that seemed to writhe around as if looking for something. He counted them and then counted them again, deciding that there were far too many to belong just to his patrol.

He struggled with indecision, not used to having to make judgement calls like this on his own. The whole situation felt like it was balancing on tenterhooks, like there was something happening that he just didn't understand. He jumped when Danny tapped him on the shoulder yet had the presence of mind not to raise his rifle – he hadn't noticed her approaching.

"What's happening? Why aren't they moving?" Danny whispered, distraught.

"I do not know. Wait." The Lukratza used his comms equipment to try and contact his patrol as quietly as he could. They could clearly hear his voice coming from multiple bodies, emanating from the radios strapped to their armour in a ghostly chorus that echoed emptily around the clearing. There was no reply or movement to imply that they had been heard. This was both a good sign and a bad one as it meant that whoever had caused the chaos hadn't paused to remain in the area – but it also meant that none of the people in the clearing was able to respond to his hails.

Danny continually scanned the area and suddenly spotted a bundle of red robes lying on the grass, right in the middle of the clearing. Without a second thought, she launched herself forwards and pelted towards what she assumed would be the body of her Master. Within seconds, she had crossed the open space and stood above the body, desperately hoping that it was someone else, someone she didn't know. She was dismayed to be proven wrong. She began bawling and collapsed on the ground next to Rhiannon, overwhelmed by a sharp pain and sense of loss that she had hoped never to feel again.

This woman, this lovely woman, had been the only person who had been kind to her ever since that monster had abducted her from her family. She really liked Rhiannon and she had thought that the feeling was mutual, her Master's patience and caring actions giving her a sense of home and comfort in a new and strange place.

Her Lukratza friend followed her into the clearing, his rifle at the ready. Despite this new flurry of activity, nothing obvious happened. No beasts came bursting out of the undergrowth to attack them and no humans opened fire with their primitive guns. He was utterly puzzled. There was nothing on this planet that should have been able to kill these people without any noise or, at the very least, an explosion – and so quickly as well!

With Danny still inconsolable next to the body of her Master, he turned away and began to try and solve the puzzle set out before him. There were three things that he needed to figure out. One, what happened to the patrol to have killed them this quietly? Two, why had their bodies fallen to the ground as if running away from the clearing, back towards the two of them? Three… why was there a shadow starting to fall over him? His instincts kicked in.

He rolled towards Danny, moving to protect her from this new threat that had sprung up behind him. His paternal nature didn't give him another choice and he intended to protect her to the best of his ability. He never made it. Without a sound, he died. His body fell to the floor with a crash, startling Danny and stopping the crying. She searched for the source of the sound and to her deep regret, found it. Another quick scan of the area showed her that there was nothing different from her last look, no immediate threat that she could see - only the freshly maimed corpse of her friend.

This was too much. Turning faster and faster on the spot, trying to keep an eye on everything around her at the same time, her brain kicked in to analysis mode and she calmed slightly.

What was she meant to do now? She was all on her own on a planet completely alien to her. She had no friends or allies and no idea how to use one of the Lukratza guns or even one of their radios. Her Master was dead. Her control of Magick was minimal and her teacher, the one who was meant to help her unlock her potential, was gone forever.

At least, she thought that Rhiannon was dead. She should really check before she worked herself up again and, thus resolved, she reached down to Rhiannon's neck to see if she could find a pulse. What she hadn't expected was for her Master to reach back to her, especially as she had stayed so deadly still whilst Danny had grieved right next to her. She started and fell on her backside, scrambling away in fearful surprise.

"Master, are you okay? What happened?" Danny asked when she had recovered her wits.

Rhiannon rose from the ground slowly, twitching and jerking in an unnatural way until she was finally upright, facing away from Danny.

"Master? Why aren't you talking to me? Do you need medical attention? Do you want me to go and find help?"

No reply. Danny was sure that something was wrong, even though she couldn't put her finger on it. It wasn't like Rhiannon to ignore her so this fact alone convinced her that the situation was beyond wrong. She reached out to Rhiannon once more, grasping her arm and pulling her around. What she saw was something that she had never imagined seeing, even in her worst nightmares. She screamed.

What she had thought was her Master coming back to consciousness was nothing of the sort. The same black liquid that was on the faces of the Lukratza was flowing down Rhiannon's face and her skin looked like it had been cracked, as if it were a glass dropped from a height or belonged to a person mummified centuries ago. There was an intelligence glinting in the older woman's eyes and Danny could feel the malevolence coming out of it even from here. Whatever had happened to Rhiannon, she wasn't the same person anymore. The thing that was using her Master's body raised an arm and pointed at Danny.

"You! You are what we have been looking for!" The deep voice that came from her Master sounded different, a cacophony of numerous people scrambling to speak all at the same time from the same mouth. The creature began ambling towards her, slowly getting used to its new body and becoming more adept with each passing moment. The arm remained raised but the hand contorted into a claw. "We have waited so long for you. You will come with us. We are hungry and you are the sustenance that we need. Only you can stop it. Only you can stop the unbearable pain."

Danny was utterly terrified and couldn't believe what she was seeing or hearing. Her juvenile mind simply wasn't prepared for a situation like this, hoping desperately that her Master was playing an awful joke on her. She couldn't understand why the older woman would do this to her so she tried to get through to her again.

"Master, stop! Why are you messing around like this? Why are you doing this to me?" She felt the power in her body begin building in response to this threat without prompt, not intimately tied into her fight or flight reaction. If she didn't release the energy, she was sure that she was going to explode. The pressure in her head grew intensely, a pressure cooker of thoughts and raw power.

The Thing kept ambling towards her with its head cocked at an unnatural angle, drawing ever closer. It moved in a shuffling motion, still unfamiliar with the layout of this body. It lost its balance on a couple of occasions, nearly falling back to the grass but regaining control at the last second. It looked for all the worlds like a zombie but that was impossible – they didn't exist except in those old, classical movies.

Danny stood rooted to the spot, unable to compute what she was seeing with her own eyes. Her body refused to acknowledge what her brain already knew – this was not her Master; this was something new, something dangerous. She tried to sort through what it had said but none of it made any sense. What did it mean, it had been waiting for her?

"Please stop," Danny pleaded through tears. "Please. I just want to go home."

"Come with us. We will take you home," the Thing said in response. The tone had changed as the Thing practised with Rhiannon's vocal cords.

As it droned its response, it reached out over the final distance to make contact with her. Danny saw that her Master's nails had cracked open and were bleeding, almost like something was trying to burst out of the skin. The Magick within Danny did not want to go anywhere with this Thing and made its move, quicker than any conscious decision that she would have been able to make by herself.

Like an outrushing tide inevitably drawing back to the beach, the power began to build again. This was like the first time, the time with the Citadel Rock but much, much stronger. Just as the Thing made the barest contact with her skin, Danny felt the energy release in a huge shockwave. A flash and bang accompanied the release and the Thing in her Master's body went flying away from her.

Danny tasted the distinctive tang of copper in her mouth and a wave of exhaustion swept over her body. As she lost consciousness, a wall of white went over her vision and she heard herself screaming; a raw, animalistic scream that she only barely recognised as her own voice.

21

CHAPTER TWENTY-ONE

This was the weirdest day that Reynolds had ever experienced, even counting the time he was nearly cooked alive at Pollux. It had started with the encounter with the Lukratza patrol that had cost Baker his arm and it had only gotten worse from there. They had been making good time back to the royal lines but for some reason, they had actually been heading in the wrong direction.

They should have been heading directly east to get where they wanted to go and they had been following the compasses in their HUDs, assuming they had been going the right way. The problem was they had been heading steadily south instead, almost making a beeline for the daunting sight of the Citadel in the distance. Although it was only visible through the trees every now and again, each time they caught a glimpse of it they knew they had veered off course once again.

Baker was ambulatory and he was stable for the moment. His head was clear enough that he was still helpful to the squad, albeit in a reduced capacity. He could hold a pistol, if not his rifle, and that was good enough to keep him busy and distracted from his problems. Reynolds' second biggest concern was attempting to get to the nearest hospital in good enough time that they may be able to reattach Baker's actual arm rather than resort to having to install a prosthetic. That now didn't look likely. The biggest worry praying on his mind was that he still hadn't made contact with headquarters despite numerous attempts to do so. Things like this were not supposed to happen; equipment that had cost millions should not just stop working of its own accord.

"Johnson, you've attended enough survival courses that even if your compass isn't working, you should be able to navigate by the sun. Why do we keep getting off course?" Reynolds' frustration boiled over and he started to take it out on his team.

"I don't know, Sarge! One minute I'm heading in the right direction then next I notice that I'm veering south without knowing why. It's like something wants us to be heading that way. I'm not familiar enough with the layout of the Midway system to navigate by the sun yet, either."

"That's ridiculous. You are in control of your actions, not some nefarious higher power that has unknown intentions. Sort it! And you've pulled some extra training when we finish this contest."

"Yes, sir." Johnson sounded embarrassed. Reynolds knew that Johnson would work twice as hard to make up for his mistake, even though Reynolds himself should have been better able to control his temper. Johnson had the good sense not to push back and point out that his Sergeant had also had the same training, knowing well that to do so would backfire badly.

That Johnson was leading the squad in the wrong direction was only one of the smaller things that had been going wrong. Three times throughout their journey they had either happened across a field full of dead Lukratza or spied live ones running away from something unknown. Reynolds wasn't sure what the unknown thing could be but there must be only a small list of possibilities. He wished he knew what was on that list. Luckily, they hadn't needed to engage any of them so there had been no further casualties. A small blessing perhaps yet one that was important to the Sergeant.

Please, for King's sake, let nothing else happen. Let us meet up with Brydges without another incident, Reynolds thought to himself only moments before a large, distant explosion shattered the relative quiet of the day.

"Where did that come from? Can anyone give me a location?" Reynolds asked the squad, his head on a swivel.

Haley was the one to provide an answer. "I'd estimate a click further south of us, sir. I was looking at it by chance. It was weird, though. There was no fireball, just an expansion of white light. I don't know of any weapons in the Lukratza arsenal that could cause anything like that."

Sinclair, Baker and Johnson agreed that they couldn't think of a probable cause and Baker said he saw the light as well (a worrying sentence considering his injuries, but one that the Sergeant let pass without comment). Reynolds thought about whether or not to investigate, his mind going back and forth with the same uncharacteristic indecision that had plagued him all day. Something like this, however, really should be looked at. It could be crucial later on and any information they could provide to the Colonel could be vitally important.

"Okay, boys and girls. Let's go see what's causing the ruckus." Reynolds ordered his squad back into motion.

I just had to think it, didn't I?

#

They didn't come across any more Lukratza until they got to where they estimated had been the epicentre of the explosion. It was a clearing that looked like it had been cut down to make space for a dropship but it wasn't obviously man- (or lizard-) made. Johnson had taken over as the vanguard since Baker was indisposed and so was the first one on site. They heard him whistle down the radio.

"You've got to get up here, sir. I can't find the words to explain it to you. It would be better if you had a look yourself."

"Copy." Reynolds spurred the squad into a faster pace, his mind awash with the possibilities. When they got to Johnson's location, what they saw hadn't even made his list.

Piles of Lukratza bodies had been carelessly thrown to the edge of the clearing, obviously moved by the release of energy from anywhere that they may have originally fallen. The trees at the edge were bending away from the epicentre of the blast and all the smaller shrubbery looked the worse for wear yet there were no fires, something which Reynolds would normally have seen had the incident been caused by explosives. There was only one thing left in the middle of the field and it was the last thing that Reynolds would ever have expected to see on this or any other battlefield.

A small, blonde and young-looking girl in the blue robes of a Mage Apprentice, perhaps a teenager at most, was on her hands and knees. Though Reynolds had no previous or personal experience with the Order, he knew all about them as did the vast majority of humans. Their exploits had been turned into so many major motion pictures and had been the subject of countless fantasy novels that he would recognise one anywhere.

The arms of her robes were in tatters and there was evidence of blood on her torso. She had been sick on the floor and was trying to crawl across the grass to what Reynolds now realised was the red-robed body of a Master. She paused to vomit again, unaware of the armoured humans now watching her. Wiping her mouth on what was left of her sleeve, she gathered her energy and started on her way to the body once more.

Reynolds directed his squad to spread out and keep a watchful eye. He was concerned that whatever had caused the blast could still be nearby and didn't want to get caught off-guard once again.

Once done he slowly approached the girl, making sure to walk in her line of sight so that she would see him coming. He didn't want to startle her and figured that she had been through enough already without a huge tank of a man scaring her out of her skin. The poor girl was clearly traumatised and she had no weapons that he could see but he knew that this could be a red herring, her position in the Order clearly giving her powers that he didn't understand. How strong she was he didn't know but he thought it better not to take the risk. Discretion was the better part of valour, after all.

He stopped a metre away from her and knelt down to get closer to her level. All the while, she was slowly, surely and painfully crawling towards the mangled body of her Master. She looked beaten, weary beyond words and only moments from giving up.

"Hey, kid," Reynolds started. Before he could go any further, the girl's head snapped up and he felt what could have been a branch collide with his helmet. He fell to the side in shock, mindful enough to keep his hands away from his rifle, hoping that this would make him less of a perceived threat to the girl. He put them up to show her that he meant no harm, either to her or to the body of the Master. He heard laughter over the network.

"Ha! Sarge got knocked onto his backside by a little girl!" Baker was still and would always be an ass.

"Eyes front, troopers! Stop gawking at me in case something nasty is about to stab you in the gut!" He really needed to have a word with Baker about staying focused. He looked over at Johnson and could tell by the way he was holding his body that he was already in intense discussion with the ne'er-do-well.

The girl had now stopped moving. She stared at Reynolds through pain-filled eyes. He wondered if she was concussed or confused. Hell, he would be in her situation. Actually, he was confused anyway.

"Hey, kid," he tried again, "what happened here? Are you alright?"

The girls took a few seconds to respond, forcing the words out as if they tasted bad. "The black goo killed everyone. It said that it had been looking for me!"

Reynolds lost all concept of getting her to make sense.

"Don't get worked up now, kiddo. We're gonna take good care of you." He slowly got back on his feet and moved closer. He saw the girl tense up as he approached and decided that he had gotten as close as he could, sinking onto his haunches in an attempt to calm the girl down. "You don't want to make anything worse. What caused the explosion?"

"The black goo tried to steal me away. I caused the explosion because I didn't want it to take me. It wasn't really me, it was the Magick."

Reynolds activated his comm. "Haley, come take a look at her. I think she's taken a hit to the head. She isn't making much sense. Saying something about the black liquid we've seen on the Lukratza talking to her."

Haley came over and bent down to take some medical readings from the girl. As soon as she touched her, the girl gave a loud and piercing scream, a look of horror plastered over her face. She passed out. A shockwave came out of her mouth, pushing Haley away before dissipating harmlessly in the jungle. The others were unaffected but Haley stumbled, just about keeping her footing.

"Damn, Sarge. We've got one of these kid magicians on our hands."

"They're called Mages, Haley. Despite how they're portrayed in the media, rumour has it that they're a good bunch of people. I have a feeling they're gonna want her back. Get her up, make her comfortable and set up a hide. We're going to rest until the afternoon and try to figure out what the hell is going on."

#

Having set up a hide large enough for the entire squad plus one smaller human, Reynolds pulled Johnson aside. Walking him away from the others, he pointed at his helmet, indicating that they should remove them. He didn't want the others overhearing their conversation because they forgot to mute their microphones.

"Johnson, I think we could be in real trouble here. Please tell me you managed to make contact with the Colonel."

"No, sir. I've been trying all day but all I get back is static. It's the same on all channels – I can't get hold of the fleet or even the Citadel. All emergency channels are blocked and none of our suits are being updated. We're being jammed."

"Damn. What do you make of the girl?"

"Not much right now, sir, considering she's still unconscious. She shouldn't be out here alone, although I suppose she wasn't if that was the body of her Master. She looks like she needs some friends." Johnson wearily mopped sweat from his forehead with his hand and looked at

Reynolds questioningly. "Maybe that's us. What are we going to do with her?"

"Well, she can't stay with us if we're going back to the Colonel and we also can't cut her loose and wish her all the best." Reynolds flung himself onto the ground and fiddled with his helmet, thoughtlessly prodding one of the attachments that had started to come loose. He was lost in thought for a few minutes, then steeled himself for his next words.

"The way it's going at the moment I don't think that linking up with the rest of the force is the best idea. We haven't heard from them for hours and we haven't seen a single sign of them. With all the weird stuff that's going on, maybe we should be thinking about asking the Mages for help. They might be able to provide an explanation. That would kill two birds with one stone – get the girl somewhere safe and help Brydges at the same time."

A burst of noise from his helmet had Reynolds scrambling to put it back on. Someone was finally trying to get in touch with them and King be damned if he was going to miss the chance to talk to another human.

"This is Sergeant Reynolds. To whom am I speaking?"

He almost threw the helmet away in frustration when the radio crackled static back at him. Just before he could release it, a tinny voice came out of the speaker.

"... request assistance. Under... from unknown... taking heavy cas-...through the trees!"

"Say again, I did not copy." He was shouting into the mic despite himself.

Nothing but crackling. The main force was clearly in trouble. Reynolds was torn between going to help them and taking the girl back to the Citadel. With all his heart he would have loved to help the Colonel but realistically he couldn't do that with a teenage girl in tow, no matter how powerful she might be. He looked to Johnson to see if he had an answer and only got a shake of the head as a reply.

"It's your call, Sarge. We'll follow you either way."

It was his decision and he had to make it. He was in charge; he alone was responsible for the wellbeing of his team. He was now also responsible for the wellbeing of the girl. He breathed deeply, calmed down and tried to think it through logically.

His decision was, in the end, not an easy one. Yet it was the only one that made sense to him. If they got the girl back to the Citadel, the Mages might be inclined to give him more information or even help him. It was a no-brainer – a favour for a favour.

"Saddle up. We need to get this girl back to where she belongs ASAP. It's the only way we might be able to help Colonel Brydges and maybe get an explanation for all this crazy shit."

22

CHAPTER TWENTY-TWO

Danny felt like she was floating. It was a feeling that she was becoming intimately familiar with. She thought, *am I dead?* She couldn't be as there was a hard pressure on her stomach which was rather uncomfortable. If she was dead then she thought that there wasn't meant to be any pain. Still, all she could see was darkness which would tally up with her being dead. It took her a few minutes to remember that opening her eyes was an option – so she did.

The first thing that she noticed was that she was upside down. She could see her arms and hands dangling in front of her, which wasn't normal. She could also see what looked suspiciously like a man's armoured butt near her head. What in the worlds?

She panicked. The last thing she could remember was a large man trying to talk to her, looking like he was encased in metal. After that – nothing. What had happened while she was out cold? She started struggling against the arms that held her in place, swinging her legs in an attempt to kick whoever was carrying her. She didn't stop to think that kicking a man in metal who had a gun could possibly be a bad idea. At this point, she was acting solely on instinct. With a sense of satisfaction, she got her aim spot on and kicked the man in the crotch. Mistake.

A sharp metallic clang was the result of her kick along with a blossoming of intense pain in her foot. The man carrying her started to laugh. He used his armour's speakers to talk to her, well-intentioned laughter booming out across the landscape.

"Let's have none of that now, miss. You're not in any danger. My name's Johnson and I'm the poor bloke who has to carry you. Let me tell you, you get quite heavy after the first hour or so. Want me to put you down?"

Danny nodded before realising that he wouldn't be able to see her doing that, mentally reprimanding herself for not keeping her wits. *Interesting,* she thought, *how much that voice correcting me sounded just like Rhiannon.* Her foot still hurt but the throbbing was lessening as the seconds passed.

"Yes, please," she said meekly, mentally with it enough to remember her manners. So, he did.

When she was once again standing on her own two feet, she took stock of her surroundings. Johnson wasn't the only man in armour – there were a total of four others. Three, actually. She noticed that one of the suits of armour was designed for a woman. Curiously, one of the men was missing his right arm, a metal plate covering the end of his stump. She wondered what had been the cause of that and then shuddered, a cold shiver going down her spine. She hoped that it wasn't something like the thing that had stolen her Master's body.

"Miss?" The largest soldier approached her, concerned that she hadn't said a word since the man called Johnson had lowered her to the ground. She thought that she recognised him as the man who had tried talking to her in the clearing. "Miss, my name is Sergeant Reynolds. This here is my squad. You've already met Johnson. The others are Haley, Sinclair and Baker. Baker's an ass, but he's 'armless."

As he mentioned each name, the body that it belonged to waved at her with varying degrees of enthusiasm. The last one tried to wave at her then remembered that it was a bit creepy to wave at a teenage girl with only half a limb. He sheepishly lowered his arm and looked at his Sergeant.

"Sarge, why do you have to make a joke out of my situation? It hurt. A lot. And I don't appreciate you making light of it." Baker realised that he had set himself up for another joke about his arm. No one had the presence of mind to take advantage of the opening; they were all focused on Danny.

"Baker – what are you?"

"An ass, sir," Baker sighed.

"That's right. Matter of fact, we all are. My squad's call sign is the Flaming Donkeys." The squad found that rather funny and broke out into laughter. It was the first time that they had been referred to as such by the Sergeant himself and they all rather liked it.

The laughter helped set Danny at ease. They seemed nice enough. She remembered her manners once more.

"Thank you for saving me, sir. My name is Danila or Danny to my friends. I don't have many friends." The quietly spoken words and the fact that the girl didn't have many friends cut straight through Reynolds' heart, but Danny wasn't aware how this was making him feel a fierce sense of protectiveness towards her.

"I think we're your friends, Danny. You don't need to thank us. You seemed like you needed some help and that's what soldiers do. We help people. You're fortunate that we were close by. Can you tell me more about what happened to you now?" Reynolds sat on the ground and motioned for Danny to do the same, removing his helmet as he did so. The rest of the team spread out and set a watch, keeping half an ear on the conversation whilst trying to look like they weren't.

Danny sat a small distance away from the Sergeant, crossing her legs in the long grass and hoping that there weren't any creepy-crawlies looking to latch onto someone. She was silent for a while, lost in the cavernous interior of her mind. When she began speaking, the words came out in a rush, a huge sense of release accompanying the verbal diarrhoea. Having started the story, she was loath to be interrupted lest she be unable to begin again and Reynolds seemed to sense this, keeping his peace and allowing her the catharsis.

She explained who she was without going into too much detail and then a bit more about what she was doing on the battlefield. She told them about the patrol leaving her to go and investigate an anomaly and she told them about getting bored and following them. She told them about the Lukratza who had been her friend and the group were struck with a sense of how unique this young woman was. None of them had ever heard of a human making friends with one of the hulking lizards before.

When she got around to describing what had happened in the clearing, however, she had to work harder to get the words out. She had been talking for so long that her throat had gone dry. After a failed attempt to moisten her lips, she asked for a drink and Reynolds handed her a water flask, from which she drank deeply before continuing.

"It's like they were all infected with something that killed them really quickly; a virus that ravages the host with no regard for its own proliferation." Reynolds was in awe of the vocabulary that the teenager was using, wondering in a flash of mischief if Baker was able to follow the conversation.

"My Master...my Master came back to life and tried to attack me. She wasn't human anymore and it scared me. I protected myself the only way I knew how. With Magick. Well, the Magick protected me, really. I just kind of... helped it. Then you guys turned up and..." She trailed off, unable to reconcile her emotions with her visage. Hot tears threatened to spill down her cheeks and she blinked them away. She wouldn't cry in front of these people, she swore to herself.

The squad maintained their silence in respect of what Danny had been through. All around them, the low-level noise that a healthy jungle with all its inhabitants made filled the space, allowing them time with their thoughts. They were all unintentionally comparing it to their own experiences and noting where they added up. It was a tale that was hard to believe and coming from anyone else, on any other day than today, they wouldn't have believed her. The silence dragged on for a time, none of them willing to break the spell and the moment's peace.

Eventually, Danny looked up at them again, her eyes gleaming with more unreleased tears. She was so very tired.

"Can you please take me back to the Citadel? I'm sure that the Masters would reward you for doing that and we really need them to deal with whatever is happening here. If anyone would know what is going on, it would be them. I need to find a way to help. I don't want to see anyone else die."

Reynolds found himself admiring the strength that Danny was displaying. As he got to know this girl, he was liking her more and more. Her personality was beginning to shine through now that she had opened up to them. He grinned at her and she immediately felt reassured.

"Of course we will. We're already en route to the Citadel." Reynolds stood up and raised his arms in a satisfying stretch. "We aren't that far away really. How are you feeling now? Any pain?"

"No, sir." It was true. Although she had come to with a headache, it was now gone – as if by Magick!

"Don't call me sir. Teenagers calling me sir makes me nervous. Call me Geoff."

Danny smiled at him. "Thanks, Geoff."

Baker piped up from the periphery. "Can I call you Geoff?"

"You're an ass, Baker."

23

CHAPTER TWENTY-THREE

The communication blackout was now system-wide. Not a single individual could speak to anyone else unless they were within shouting distance. The civilian population of Midway went about their business as normally as possible with short-range communication still available in their cities. Only those who were religiously watching the Dùbhlan seemed to notice that something was amiss, although their complaints were mostly ignored as the holo-shows displayed replay after replay of old skirmishes.

The Lukratza fleet was trying to make contact with their troops in a calm, collected and professional manner, whilst the H.M.S. *Excellence* was powering back to Midway, Admiral Leystrom and General Webb both ranting at the crew to re-establish contact. Neither group would be successful in their aims.

On the planet, pandemonium reigned. The human assault had been splintered into smaller groups, each separate and isolated from the others. All were trying to make sense of what was happening, again unsuccessfully. One by one, troops fell to the mysterious black shadows until the only ones remaining were Colonel Brydges with his command staff and Sergeant Reynolds and Danny who were heading to the Citadel.

Brydges was subjected to a relentless hunt and his staff gave their lives to keep him moving. The Shadows knew that he was in charge of the remaining humans and wanted to take his knowledge for their own. At that very moment, he was staring up at the azure sky, blood pouring down his chest from a shoulder injury as he listened to his troops screaming in pain and wondering what the fuck was happening.

Things fared no better for the Lukratza. They were being chased through the jungle, killed and mutilated by something they could neither see nor comprehend. Air patrols crashed on the surface as their operators died in agony, scarring the face of Midway further. The Lukratza commander made a desperate last stand, his troop's weapons ineffective against the shadows. He died, cowering in a corner against his nature, unable to control anything around him at the last. Nothing even remotely similar to this had ever happened at a Dùbhlan before and the commander was unable to comprehend the series of events.

In their cage at the airfield on the south end of the line, the Lukrog saw that their handlers were gone and began attacking the metal sheeting holding them in, bellowing in frustration and hunger.

Satisfied that nothing left on the field could summon enough strength to challenge them, the black Shadows turned their attention to the Citadel. In all its history, it had not once been attacked. This was about to change. Only one Mage knew what the shadows were, knew truly. Sure, the rest of them knew the rumours, knew that there was something that could change their reality. The Lord Regent had all the information. It had been handed down from Lord Regent to Lord Regent since the founding of the Order and with this knowledge came fear. He knew what they were after. He sensed the change and his head swung up from the reports he was reading, gazing directly in the direction Danny would be coming from.

They wanted Danny. They wanted the strongest source of Magick they had felt for millennia. They thought she was at the Citadel. The Shadows marched to war. They were hungry.

24

CHAPTER TWENTY-FOUR

Despite the insane events that they had experienced over the last day and the fact that they had been awake for most of those twenty-four hours, Reynolds and his team were now firmly awake. Trained to deal with the unexpected, what was happening was even still beyond them but they were determined to make a difference and to come out of the other end of it alive and well – although not necessarily in one piece. They knew little of what was truly happening but they were prepared to die to escort Danny back to the Citadel, hoping that an intervention from the Order would be enough to restore some sanity to this incomprehensible situation.

The number of bodies they saw on their route march was beyond count. Nothing had attacked them as of yet but they kept their guard up even so. Danny had begun that march keeping to herself, quietly trying to make sense of what had happened to her and her Master. She knew that the Lord Regent – and Master Rhiannon – had thought that she could be a powerful Mage but the reaction she had gained from the thing that had taken over her Master's body made her think there was more to it. If only she had been on Midway for longer or had spent more of her free time in the archives, perhaps she would know more! Perhaps then she would understand!

As the day wore on, Danny started to come out of her shell and engage with the others. She began questioning Johnson about his equipment, where he had been and what he had seen. Only she would have been able to draw the parallel to the patrol she had been on earlier that day, had she been attentive enough to draw the comparison.

Johnson had taken a liking to the girl, indulging her curiosity with a patience that had been reserved only for members of his team in the past. He rather liked her, something that Reynolds had noted with wry amusement and no small sense of relief, saving Reynolds himself from having to play chaperone.

The girl had a very endearing personality and seemed to engender good feelings from everyone around her. Reynolds had never married or had a family so he was a little unsure about how to interact with Danny, meaning that he was glad that Johnson was taking point on this one. For his entire career, his squad had been his family and he had never expected that to change.

The jungle passed them by without notice as they hiked for miles under the glaring sun. They knew that they were getting close to the edge of the permitted battlefield and wondered what would be waiting for them at the boundary.

To the best of Reynolds' knowledge, no one had ever tried to penetrate beyond the edge of the field, perhaps worried about the severity of the response from the Order and the Hegemony. Rumour had it that there were combat droids patrolling the perimeter, ready to dole out swift punishment to any encroachers. Other rumours said that the Mages relied on their reputation to stop anyone from transgressing away from the contest. With no solid examples of previous attempts, there was simply no way to know. This would be another first for the Flaming Donkeys (damn, even Reynolds was mentally referring to himself by that ridiculous name now!).

One thing they did know was that they were nearing the point where they would start to get some answers. They had just gone through the southern-most Lukratza base without any problems. They had approached it as stealthily as they could, two of them going forward to scout the area. They had reported back to Reynolds that the base was deserted so they had re-joined the squad and together they had swiftly walked past the scenes of carnage that had awaited them.

As they were going through the base, Haley had signalled for them to stop and they quickly knelt down in stable firing positions, their rifles oscillating backwards and forwards on the search for targets. Danny had taken a position behind Johnson, using his body as a shield in case she was the target. She had done this by instinct – they hadn't pre-agreed what she would do were they to encounter trouble but she thought it best to take cover. Johnson silently thought that she was doing the right thing and adjusted his body to cover her just that little bit more.

Although her mental shield was still in place, she hadn't thought about using Magick since coming back to reality on Johnson's shoulder. Its silken and persuasive voice was still whispering to her but she had mostly been ignoring it, preferring instead to focus on getting to know the people who had saved her life.

"Sarge, I can hear a banging. If the base is as clear as we thought it was, there shouldn't be anything left to make that noise." Haley sounded worried. It took a lot to shake Haley but the story that Danny had woven for them had her on edge.

"True. Fan out and find the source of that noise but do not make contact unless it becomes absolutely necessary," Reynolds ordered. The squad separated into pairs and went off to investigate, leaving Reynolds alone with Danny.

"What do you think it is?" Danny asked, only now realising that this was the very base she had inspected with Rhiannon at the start of the day. *Was it only really this morning?*

"Knowing the Lukratza, it could be absolutely anything." Reynolds didn't think he sounded particularly reassuring. Damn, he needed more practise at this.

They were standing there for only a few moments before Sinclair's voice came over the comms. "Sarge, we found the source. Looks like three of those big beasts locked in a cage with each other. They're going mental, trying to break out. What do you want me to do?"

"They're called Lukrog," Danny interjected quickly, realising that the information she had from her previous visit would turn out to be incredibly useful. It looked so very different without the Lukratza running around the base like headless chickens; almost peaceful. Peaceful, that is, without the Lukrog going nuts.

Reynolds looked at her for a second and then said, "Huh... the more you know, I guess. Know anything about how to kill them?"

"Sorry but no. We didn't go into too much detail. We got close to them but they scared me a lot and one of them spat at my Master. The Lukratza did mention something about a fail-safe... What's a fail-safe?"

"It's supposed to be a way to make sure that something dangerous can't hurt you when it's not supposed to. Sometimes it goes wrong though and the thing does the damage anyway." Reynolds answered in an off-hand way, already planning their next move.

The squad stood captivated by the sight of the raging Lukrog until Reynolds shook the cobwebs out of his head and brought them all back to reality.

"Fall in, all of you. They're obviously trying to escape and we definitely don't want to be here when they do. Let's get a move on and get out of the area as quickly as possible."

#

It was well past noon now and they were making good progress away from the base. It wasn't long, however, before disaster nearly struck at the team and prevented them from ever getting close to the Citadel. Reynolds had been waiting for something, anything to happen to them and he was annoyed to be proven correct. As the sun began its slow descent towards the distant horizon, the team had their closest encounter with a Shadow to date.

The first they knew about it was once again the presence of corpses. They didn't slow down to check on them though, as they had become so used to seeing bodies on the field, each clearly dead and with no hope of coming back. The risk was simply too high to attempt anything heroic. This would have seemed like a heartless choice to an outside observer but they had decided not to waste time on the off-chance that they found a survivor simply because the odds of finding one were so slim. Rushing through the field of bodies, Haley tripped over an outlying arm and took a second to recover, staring up at the sky and catching her breath.

"Haley, everything all right?" Reynolds asked. The team had come to a halt and stood waiting expectantly for her to regain her footing.

"Yeah, Sarge, I'm fine. Just need a breather, is all." After a short time, Haley stood back up and then pointed behind the team and shouted, "Behind you!"

They swivelled, caught so off-guard by Haley's fall that they hadn't thought to keep watch over the area. Danny was the first to spot what Haley had been pointing at and screamed. There was one of the Shadows, gently floating out from behind a tree. The squad reacted in the only way they knew how – they opened fire.

Quickly opening gaps between each other to minimise the risk of being hit all at once, they poured rounds at their target which seemed unaffected by the sheer amount of lead coming its way. Danny stood rooted to the spot, eventually realising that staying where she was would do neither her nor her friends any favours.

The Shadow gained speed and picked a target. It started moving quickly towards Sinclair who had enfiladed to the left, hoping to gain some cover behind a tree and find a more stable firing platform.

Reynolds had an idea and wondered if it would work. "Change rounds! Taser rounds only!"

The squad made the switch in the blink of an eye and continued firing but the new Taser rounds had no effect beyond electrifying a poor, small lizard that had been sunning itself on a branch. Clearly braver than others of its kind, the lizard hadn't taken flight like the rest of the wildlife, instead, making the most of the opportunity to get a good spot. When the Taser round hit, it ran for its life, deeply regretting staying behind.

Undeterred, the Shadow closed on Sinclair. He scrambled backwards until his back hit the trunk of the tree he had been aiming for and was trapped and unable to move anywhere else. The Shadow touched his helmet in a gentle, almost loving way but the reaction from Sinclair was well out of proportion to the caress.

A black liquid had dropped out of the Shadow and landed on his helmet, prompting the soldier to start rolling in the grass to try and get rid of the thing. He was partly successful, mainly because the Shadow just stood there and watched him as if amused by his attempts to escape.

With the liquid now on the grass rather than on his helmet, Sinclair faced up to the Shadow and drew his combat knife, trying something else that none of the team had tried yet. It was not a good idea. As the blade plunged into the Shadow, more of the black liquid seeped out of the shadow and was now attached to his arm.

The Shadow, however, had taken exception to Sinclair's stabbing attempt and decided that it had had enough fun with him. The arm came up again, still going for his helmet but this time with much more speed. When it connected, Sinclair went flying away in the direction of the slap. The speed he was travelling at caused the liquid on his arm to fortuitously slip from his armour. He connected head first with another tree, causing a sickeningly loud bang before sliding down the tree to come to a rest near the roots.

Danny was aghast. The Shadows had taken her Master and she would be damned before allowing it to take another person she cared about and who cared about her. The squad was caught between trying to drive their opponent away and trying to go and check on the lifeless form of Sinclair and Danny knew that saving all of their lives might be a task that only she could do.

The Magick whispered that perhaps they could do something together and Danny allowed it to swell within her chest. Thinking outside the box, she made a shield as she had been taught but applied it in a completely different way. First, she shielded herself. Then, she stretched it outside her body until it had moulded itself to her shape. Finally, she aimed the shield at her target and threw it. Her aim was true.

The Shadow was trapped. Danny had built the shield but then used it to fence in the inky blackness, not allowing it to break free and move. The squad were staring at what was happening, their guns hanging limply by their sides as the change in circumstance became evident.

Danny ignored them, knowing that there wasn't nearly enough time to explain and already breathing heavily from her exertions in this battle of wills. As the Shadow, with increasing frustration and fury, attempted to escape from the minute prison that Danny had erected for it, she had to apply more power to the Magick to keep it trapped.

"Go! Get Sinclair and move! I can't hold it for long!" The strain was evident in her voice and Reynolds decided there and then that he wouldn't look a gift horse in the mouth.

Not needing another prompt, Reynolds himself sprinted over to Sinclair and threw him over his shoulder, the rest of the squad following. They disappeared into the jungle and Danny followed them, walking backwards and never taking her eyes off the Shadow. Step by step, she increased the distance between herself and her prisoner and it felt like forever before the leaves from the trees appeared in her peripheral vision. The amount of power she needed to maintain the makeshift prison increased with each step back and Danny knew it was only a matter of time before the strength left her entirely.

As soon as she noticed a tree trunk sliding past her as she moved backwards, she turned away from the Shadow and ran after the squad, her mind and power still in the clearing behind. The Shadow let loose a fearsome scream of frustration and Danny felt it increase its struggle against the shield-prison.

After ten minutes, the requirement was too great and Danny dropped the shield, gulping down the fresh air to try and cool her massively overheating body. Reynolds looked askance at her but she shook her head, not wanting to talk about the grim fate that they had almost met.

"That was close," Reynolds stated, struggling to catch his breath. He thought it would be best to stop everyone from dwelling on their close call so he spurred them onwards and hoped it would distract them. "Let's keep moving; we've got a long way to go still."

He turned and looked squarely at the person who had saved them.

"Danny. Thank you."

The squad chorused their agreement and they continued on their way, each lost in their own minds, each thinking about the loved ones that they were very nearly separated from.

25

CHAPTER TWENTY-FIVE

They were walking into new territory - at least for the squad. The jungle became denser the further away from the Lukratza base they went, a physical barrier that was making it hard for them to keep moving forward. Sinclair and Haley were right at the front, using their combat knives to hack through the undergrowth to try and provide a walkway for the rest of the team. Knowing that they were all incredibly tired, Reynolds made sure to switch the two at the front so that they all took it in turns to do this labour-intensive work.

The only person that wasn't asked to cut a path was Danny as she was clearly far too tired to be of much use and her small frame wouldn't have had the leverage to clear a path without a suit of their power armour. She offered to help twice but each time, Reynolds turned her down, figuring that she should save her energy in case they had to run or fight.

Reynolds was concentrating so deeply on hacking away the obstacles that it took him a second or two to notice that the trees had simply stopped. His arm swung through a downwards stroke without encountering any resistance, the knife clanging harmlessly against his leg plate. He raised his head and saw an open space about twenty metres long that ended in a wall that simply shouldn't have been there.

The wall stretched out as far as he could see in either direction, a clear demarcation line between the accepted violence of the battlefield and the grounds of the Citadel. Using the zoom function in his HUD, he scanned down the length of the wall, looking for a way through. After a few seconds of searching, he found a potential option.

There was an opening for a door in the wall that looked like reinforced metal, its darker colour making it more noticeable than the lighter metal of the wall itself. They couldn't tell from their current position whether the door was open or not. The wall was ten feet high and from their perspective, on the outside, it looked like it had a firing step although it was hard to be sure.

All the fanciful stories about the deterrents used by the Order went out of his head as Reynolds took stock of the situation. Out of everything wild and outlandish that he had imagined, something as benign as a wall seemed like a let-down. He was incredibly disappointed.

With the Order's political standing throughout the Hegemony and their proficiency in using Magick, they clearly felt confident enough in their powers to only put a minor obstacle in the way. They were using their reputation as a deterrent and he assumed that it must have been efficient in the past. Reynolds wondered what would happen if someone was serious about getting to the other side. Something dangerous, he was sure. He hoped that they weren't about to be the first to find out.

"Hello? Is there anyone there? We need to get to the Citadel; can someone please open the gate?" He was shouting through the armour's external speakers, his voice sounding much meeker than he had hoped. He waited for a verbal reply or some other sign of movement, not really sure what he was expecting to happen.

He looked over at Danny, tilting his helmet questioningly but she only shook her head at him. She hadn't been here long enough to know the general procedures of the Order, especially something like this which she hadn't thought to ask about in the short time she had been on the planet.

He tried again, louder and more confident. "Can anyone hear me?"

Nothing.

Johnson pointed. "The door's open, Sarge. I don't think it should be open…"

Think it through, man, Reynolds thought. *Why is the door open and why is nobody responding to me? Cutting out all the other possibilities would mean that the Shadows got here before we did. Do I just walk through the door as if nothing is wrong, or do I try and scale the wall, go over in a way they aren't expecting?* He made his decision quickly, though not without a small amount of consternation.

"Boys and girls, we all know something isn't right here. I know that we're all tired but we need to do this by the book or we'll only be making things worse for ourselves. Line up next to the door and prepare to breach. I'll count to three and when I do, I want Sinclair to throw a flashbang through the doorway and we'll all follow it through just like we've practised."

They moved to the door with a strong sense of purpose, lining up on one side of the door as it was impossible to get around to the other without being seen by whatever was through the opening. So organised, Reynolds raised his hand and lifted three fingers before slowly lowering one, then two and finally the third.

Sinclair threw a flashbang through the aperture, waited for the explosion and then the squad moved through, checking their corners as they went. There was nothing on the other side – nothing alive, anyway.

After making sure that they weren't in any immediate danger, Reynolds turned his attention to what were clearly more bodies. There were three wearing the red robes of a Master and a further seven wearing the green robes of Mages. They were arrayed in a neat semi-circle, all looking as if they had been in the process of turning away from the wall, preparing to run. He had never heard of a Mage running before but understood the deep sense of terror that the Shadows could engender.

"There's no one alive here, Sarge," Johnson reported morosely, Danny sticking close to his heels. She took one look at the bodies and promptly vomited; the memory of her Master was still fresh and raw in her mind and the sight of the corpses had dragged her feelings back to the surface even though she had been doing her level best to suppress them.

"Haley, try and figure out if any of them are still alive, but, for King's sake, don't touch them!" He pivoted quickly on the spot as he noticed movement out of the corner of his eye but all he saw was Danny straightening after her sudden attack of sickness. By the King, he was getting twitchy.

Haley had completed her quick inspection of the bodies and made her report.

"They're all dead, Sarge. The kids too."

"We're losing ground on the Shadows, then." Reynolds sighed. Against his better judgement, he'd hoped that they would get to the Citadel before their unknowable foe. If this new enemy had gotten this far, maybe they'd made it to the bastion of the Order itself.

They could clearly see the Citadel now, much larger than it had been for them before. It was a massive construct, built as much for practicality as it was for intimidation. The light coming off of the setting sun had set the Citadel ablaze and the squad looked at it in awe; that was, until they saw movement on the battlements. The awe turned into dismay as the last vestiges of their hope washed up against the huge stone bricks that had guarded the Order for centuries.

"Sarge, is that...?" Baker was lost for words. He fell to his knees and stared at the scene laid out before him.

"Yeah, Baker. It is." Reynolds knew exactly what he meant.

Strung along the battlements and clearly visible in the few courtyards that could be seen from this elevation were flashes of light and sound. The Order was in a battle for its life – and it was losing. Mages were running away from the black Shadows, so visible because the contrast between the colourful Mages and the darkness that seemed to suck in all light was stark.

As the squad stood there and watched with an all-consuming sense of dread, a small green figure fell from the edge of the wall and plummeted, gaining speed with each passing second. It was a small mercy that they didn't see it connect with the ground but the outcome was never in doubt. When flesh fell onto unyielding stone there was only ever one winner.

Danny gasped and hid her head behind her hands. Johnson saw how distraught she was and moved to comfort her, the image of a huge armoured man protectively hugging a teenage girl nearly breaking the team out of their stupor and eliciting a morbid chuckle out of Sinclair. Out of respect for Danny, the squad didn't join in, instead, allowing her some space to deal with what she was seeing.

Reynolds knelt on the ground and used his HUD to magnify the top of the tower. If the person in charge of the Order was like any other autocrat throughout history, his personal space would be in the main spire – symbolically and literally above everyone else.

"Danny, can I assume that the leader of the Order will be at the top of the Citadel?"

"That man is called the Lord Regent. Would you expect a monster like that to be anywhere else?" The strength of the hate in the teenager's voice took Reynolds by surprise. He glanced at her out of the corner of his eye before focusing again on the higher reaches of the Citadel.

As his eyes went further up the bastion, it seemed as if normality reigned on high, so far as he could tell. In the short time that the squad continued to look, unable to tear their eyes away, evidence of the Shadows progressing higher presented itself.

"It won't be long before the bigwigs at the top are in the fight along with their lackeys," Reynolds said. "We have to get there before it's too late and there's no longer anyone left to help us."

He stood back up and ordered the squad to fall in. They did so and he stood there looking at them, a feeling of pride surging through his body. They were a good team – his team – and he knew that the next few hours would be a desperate battle against time. He grinned. He was confident that they could do it.

"We're almost there. This is the final push. We've lost contact with all other human forces and we haven't seen anything alive for the whole afternoon. I don't know what these Shadows are but they are clearly more advanced than anything in the Hegemony. It's a good thing the Hegemon decided to invite the Imperial Forces to Midway when he did, otherwise, he wouldn't stand a chance." He stopped as Haley whooped and raised a fist. When she realised that she was the only one doing so, she sheepishly lowered her arm and stood silently, waiting for Reynolds to continue.

A small wind began stirring around Reynolds, causing some scattered debris to dance around him. He noticed a look of concentration on Danny's face and knew what she was doing but decided not to mention it yet, lest he spoil the moment.

"We need to get Danny back to the Citadel and we need to find out exactly what it is we're facing. You are the finest men and women I have ever served with. If anyone in the Empire can do this, we can. So, check your armour and ammo, ladies and gentlemen. Once we go in, there's no turning back. Death or glory!" Reynolds shouted the last words and was gratified when his friends and comrades shouted it back to him, all of them pumping their fists in the air. Even little Danny joined in, overwhelmed by the emotion in Reynolds' voice.

"Death or glory! Death or glory! Death or glory!"

26

CHAPTER TWENTY-SIX

Standing guard over Midway for centuries, the gargantuan castle that was the Citadel had been perpetually shrouded in mystery to the innumerable inhabitants of the galaxy, always a popular topic of movies and novels. Before the Order began its life as an organised association of users of Magick, there had been no real collaboration between the few and gifted people who had control of this one particular talent.

Each race produced a small number of Magick users and they had guarded them jealously, rarely allowing them out of their control. They were typically contained by the governments of their respective species, only brought out when they could contribute to a goal or assault a target that was proving to be difficult to crack. As time went on, the users of Magick collectively became ever more powerful and began to converse in secret, plotting a way to escape the life of servitude that fate had given them. New powers were discovered that allowed them to communicate with each other in secret, collaborating and sharing information for a common goal.

There arose a member of the same species as the Hegemon all those years later – the name of the species is never spoken aloud for fear of the government cracking down on nay-sayers, accusing them of breaking the law by speaking poorly of the reigning monarch. He united the Magickal peoples under one banner, the years of working in the shadows having borne fruit as they stood up as one person and said – no more!

After a short period of conflict – completely catastrophic to the reigning government - the Hegemony realised that staying on good terms with these people would be in their best interests, powerful as they were, and offered to negotiate in good faith. The group of Magick users agreed and a conference was convened on the capital planet of Harodia.

The Hegemon at the time was a clever creature and a brilliant diplomat. He knew that further conflict would result in the end of his rule and was canny enough to realise that he needed to compromise – he only had to persuade the Magick users that they could work together. Through negotiations with the leaders of the rebels, including the one that would go on to become the first Lord Regent, a plan was agreed that would benefit all.

Magickal users from across the galaxy gathered on Harodia, uneasy about the prospect of being in one place at the same time lest the Hegemon should destroy them in one fell swoop. What they were to hear would pleasantly surprise them and set the Hegemony on a course that it would hold for an age.

The conference started. The Hegemon was first to speak. His rhetoric was so convincing, so charismatic that his suggestions were acclaimed by the oppressed people and an agreement was reached swiftly, with little changed from the original proposal.

The Order was founded. A Lord Regent was selected and the users of Magick came together in harmony to learn, practice and live a life of contemplation, each to their own. The set-up of the organisation had barely changed since its founding, the rules and regulations that were agreed upon continuing to work long into the future. The only thing left to do was find the Order a home.

After much deliberation and a lot of scouting for potential locations, the Hegemon offered the Order a seat on one of the most famous planets in the Milky Way – Midway. Historically the site of the annual combat contest called the Dùbhlan, there was something missing from the competition that made it a tense and controversial affair - impartial judges.

The Order gratefully accepted the offer of setting up a home on Midway and so they migrated from across the galaxy, working together over a number of years to construct the Citadel, imagined as the ultimate bastion of knowledge and a refuge from the outside worlds. Eschewing the use of modern construction machinery, the massive stones were carved by hand as a labour of love and moved into place through the cooperation of the newly made Mages.

Year by year, the Citadel took shape, the Order growing into its new duties as arbitrators and keepers of the planet. When construction was finished, the Hegemon was jealous. It was unassailable by conventional means with only a strong Magickal user having even the remotest chance of conquering such a stronghold. He wondered if he had made a mistake by elevating the Order into a position of power but was to be proven wrong – time and time again, the Order would prove to be one of the Hegemony's strongest allies.

Where once they had been oppressed and controlled, the Hegemony now relied upon the Order to be the voice of reason in diplomatic disputes throughout its territory. Where their ability to mediate failed, the Mages were proficient enough in the physical applications of Magick that they could take to the battlefield to force a resolution through more permanent and sometimes final means. Over time, the governments that made up the Hegemony learned that if the Order was involved in a problem, it would be solved in the Hegemony's favour one way or another.

The Citadel itself stood unchanging for centuries, the only differences being the people who inhabited the centre of Magick. Through the myths and legends built among the dispersed populations of the galaxy, their reputation grew ever greater with each passing crisis. They were untouchable and they knew it. Concern for the greater good began to fade and was slowly replaced with an arrogance and feeling of entitlement as the reason for the existence of their Order faded in the galaxy's collective memory. Each successive generation became stronger and more involved in the day-to-day politics around them until there was no one left who could challenge them.

They had never been attacked. They had never lost a battle that they had been asked to intervene in. They had never felt the sense of vulnerability that so many regular citizens felt every single day.

That was about to change. The Citadel was about to fall.

27

CHAPTER TWENTY-SEVEN

Six humans - five with armour and one without - ran for the Citadel, not worrying so much now about being careful but trying to reach their target as quickly as possible. As they went, Reynolds made a mental note to talk to Danny about what had happened when he'd been giving his speech but as it wasn't urgent, it could wait for a time. All the while, they were expecting something bad to happen, an attack or distraction that caused them to lose time or people. Nothing happened and Reynolds grew uneasy.

The Citadel loomed ever large above them as they came closer to their destination. Sprinting across the carefully manicured grounds made it hard for the team to talk to one another and they moved in silence, eyes constantly darting left to right, and then back. The fighting continued above as the noise from the duelling caused a ruckus that rose into an assault on the ears and easily drowned out any other sound as they drew closer.

Danny struggled to keep up at first but then began to intuitively and subconsciously use the power she carried to refresh her limbs and soon she threatened to overtake the squad. The Magick was talking louder to her now, not whispering insidiously as it once had. Knowing that it was in closer proximity to the Shadows, it wanted to take control away from Danny but she kept it at bay. This constant battle within her own mind was exhausting and she knew that she would have to find a way to live in harmony with the voice before either it took control or she lost her abilities.

Recognising that getting to the Citadel before the trained soldiers was probably a bad idea, she fell back into the middle of the group and sustained the pace. Reynolds looked at her enviously. He wasn't getting any younger.

Their earlier expectations of being greeted by people who were alive (if not welcoming) had faded and they now expected the worst. It was something that Reynolds had drummed into them in every step of their training with him. Plan for the worst and hope for the best was a good mantra to live by, especially for professional soldiers.

They reached the base of the Citadel. It towered above them and Johnson whistled in awe at the sheer size of it. As the squad approached the base of the monstrous construct, they saw a large hangar-like door set into the base of the structure and adjusted their trajectory to head straight towards it, barely losing momentum. In normal, more peaceful times, the door would have remained shut to allow the work within to stay private. Mages and Masters would have left the Citadel by one of the more easily accessible courtyards to go to their next meeting or assignment. This was far from a normal time.

The hangar door was wide open and Reynolds wasn't surprised to see bodies littering the area – not just those in coloured robes but also those in what could be considered to be the normal fashion of the time. These were the dockhands, the air traffic controllers and the mechanics, all caught by surprise doing their day-to-day jobs. They weren't trained in combat and were never expected to face conflict of any sort. They were, in short, normal people and they had been slaughtered where they stood without any resistance. It was a tragedy, yet it wasn't the only tragedy to have occurred that day. Nor did Reynolds think that it would be the last.

With Danny now almost accustomed to the sight of corpses, the squad pelted straight past them heading into the building. A faint sense of nausea threatened and she swallowed sharply, keeping the contents of her stomach where they belonged.

Whatever lighting had illuminated the area beforehand had been diminished, leaving the cavernous space dark. The squad switched their HUDS over to infrared and continued moving. None of them stopped to wonder if the infrared would pick up the Shadows and they made their way through the darkness unaware of this potential hazard.

"Which way?" Reynolds asked breathlessly, the day's exertions taking their toll.

Danny took a second to think about it and then pointed directly towards one of the back corners of the hangar. "I think it's that way. There's a gravity lift that goes up to the dormitory and cafeteria area but I don't know if it'll still be working. I don't know if there are any stairs – I had no need to use them whilst I was here."

"Okay, let's have a look-see." Barely slowing down, the squad again changed course and moved in the direction that Danny had pointed. The bodies were getting thicker and more numerous. It seemed as if the workers who had been at the back of the hangar had taken notice of the furore towards the main doors and tried to run but to no avail.

Danny felt more scared than she ever had. She remembered how full of life this room had been when she had passed through with Rhiannon, even at the ridiculously early time of their visit. She desperately hoped that she wouldn't see the bodies of the two workers she had overheard gossiping about the Dùbhlan. Maybe they had finished their shift and left to go home before this had kicked off. Maybe. She bit her bottom lip to help ward off the tears that threatened to spill onto her cheeks yet again.

"Sarge, there's the lift!" Baker shouted. He was struggling more than the others, his rifle grasped in his only remaining hand. He had lost a lot of blood but was insistent that he could keep up, his determination and grit setting a brilliant example to the rest of the squad. He hadn't asked for any help so far and was dead set against asking at all. He would not be a burden, he promised himself. Reynolds made another mental note that he would position Baker in a safer area, should one be found.

"How does it work?" Reynolds was looking around for a call button or some physical control that would make sense to a soldier like him.

"You just…step into it. It takes you where you want to go. I think it reads your mind to figure out which level you want to go to. Either that or it reads your Magick." Danny hoped that it wasn't Magick, else the squad would have to find a stairway.

"Like this?" Reynolds stepped into the lift, which began emanating a light purple beam in response.

"Yeah, like that."

"Why aren't I moving?"

"Oh, I think I know why, Sarge." Sinclair reached down and grabbed the dead arm of a mechanic who could have been the last person alive in the hangar before their arrival. He dragged the body out of the way and as it cleared the lift, Reynolds suddenly shot up into the air. He quickly disappeared.

Baker winked at Danny, trying to lighten the mood and lift their spirits. "Well, that's gotten rid of him!" Danny giggled.

"I can still hear you, Baker. Follow me up, one at a time. I'm still moving so this must be one hell of a lift shaft."

"Copy, Sarge." Johnson pushed Baker towards the lift and the clang of metal on metal made Danny jump.

"Why do I have to go next?"

"Do I really need to answer that question, Baker? It's your turn in the magic space elevator. Let me know if you make it to the top still in one piece. And don't land on the Sarge, he'll only be pissed at you."

"Fine." Baker sighed again. "See you at the top, guys. Don't leave me alone with the Sarge." Baker jumped headfirst into the lift and was soon out of sight.

Danny heard him over the squad's comms.

"Whee! Oh, this is fun. It's just like flying!"

To continue Baker's poor luck, it transpired that landing on Reynolds was exactly what he did. To be fair to him, Reynolds had been close to the exit at the top of the lift and Baker didn't have much control over his movements. A large crash shattered the eerie peace as Baker smacked headfirst into his Sergeant.

"For King's sake, Baker! I thought you had more grace than that!"

"Grace, sir? I've got lots of it." Baker wasn't entirely sure what grace meant. He intended to look it up if he survived the situation. Not the smartest, he still had one of the best work rates in the squad.

"Get out of the way! The others will be coming out in a second." With some difficulty, they disentangled themselves and moved out of the way. They made the move just in time as the others began popping out of the lift in quick succession, the torches from their helmets helping to illuminate the dark space and showing them a scene that could have come directly out of a horror holo.

The corridor in which they found themselves was in much the same shape as the hangar. Bodies were littered around and the only natural light was coming from the windows, which was to say barely any at all with the sun as close to the horizon as it was.

Danny alone out of the group landed gracefully, almost like a cat falling from a height. She brushed off the front of her robes to cover the embarrassment she felt on the squad's behalf and the smile that flitted across her face and quickly gained her bearings. "This way."

The squad set off. They worked their way up the Citadel, going past rooms that had been full of life and energy when Danny had gone through them only twelve hours or so ago. The odd corpse spoiled the otherwise peaceful journey. As they got closer to the cafeteria that Danny had mentioned to the squad, the number of corpses once again increased.

That's odd, Danny thought as she noticed that some of the bodies weren't dressed in the signature robes of the Order. *I didn't notice any staff up here beforehand. Maybe they were lucky enough to get this far away from the hangar without dying. Some luck, though…*

The quiet was broken only by Haley or Sinclair frequently announcing "clear!" as they checked around corners for threats. Reynolds had been acknowledging the announcement each time but as they kept moving, he was getting out of breath again and presently began only grunting in response.

Danny pointed to a large door at the end of the corridor, this time without the two apprentices on guard, drawing Reynolds's attention.

The cafeteria was in complete disarray. It was here that the largest number of Masters had pulled together, perhaps intending to use the large space as a bulwark against the encroaching darkness. They would have been warned of the danger by the sounds coming from below – they certainly would have felt the horror of their comrades.

They had arranged the tables to create makeshift barricades and most of the bodies, from all races present in the Order, were clustered behind these. The red robes of the Masters were more prominent near the tables with the other colours further towards the back. The Masters had clearly tried to protect the lesser-developed members of the Order and had paid for their chivalry with their lives.

The squad stood there contemplatively for a short time and then pushed the vision of carnage to the back of their minds, continuing on their way with firm resolve. None of them said a word, understanding that it was only going to get worse the further up the Citadel they progressed. At some point in the journey, Baker had disposed of his rifle; he was finding it too cumbersome to allow him to keep up with the others. He drew his sidearm and kept the pace.

They were now going through the dormitory spaces. Danny was full of dread at the thought of going past her room and even more so about going past Rhiannon's. She nudged Reynolds on the shoulder and whispered, "If we get a chance, do you mind if we stop at my Master's room? I'd like to have a quick look around, try and remember her as she was and not as the monster that took her over."

"Of course. We haven't got long though, so make it quick." Reynolds was sure that his voice sounded too emotional but he had done a good job keeping it as normal as possible. As the leader, he had to contain his feelings as best he could because anything he said or did would be noticed by the team and could distract them at just the wrong moment.

He felt pity for Danny – not because she was pitiful but because he was sorry that she had had to go through all of this at such a young age. In contrast, he also marvelled that she was continuing to show a stoic face to the world, not allowing it to knock her down.

They stopped at the room that Danny pointed out as belonging to Rhiannon. She gently pushed the door open and made her way into the room, leaving the others outside to take a quick breather. The room was bare. There was no mess so she was sure that nothing bad had happened in this room. It must have been exactly as Rhiannon had left it and she was glad about that.

The last rays of the setting sun cast a faint light on a bunch of peonies in a vase on the utilitarian desk set against the window. Danny hadn't known that her Master had liked flowers. The placement of the vase, however, made her think that they had special meaning to her. With nothing else obviously jumping out at her or taking her fancy, Danny crossed the room to the desk and plucked one of the peonies from the bouquet. She slid it into her hair, just above her ear.

A single tear rolled down her cheek and she wished she'd had longer to get to know Rhiannon. She had felt like she had made a lifelong friend and mentor in the woman who had taken her under her wing and was devastated that she had been ripped away from her in such a brutal and thoughtless manner. She looked around the room and committed everything to memory.

The sun set below the horizon, bringing night to the planet of Midway. With nothing left for her to do, Danny turned and walked back through the door into the corridor. She took a deep breath, looked at Reynolds and said, "I'm ready."

28

CHAPTER TWENTY-EIGHT

They encountered no opposition on the rest of their journey. Each step towards their final destination played havoc with their nerves. As they went through empty courtyards and barren corridors, the in-built lighting became progressively worse, forcing them to rely more and more on either their torches or their infrared sensors. Dust stirred up in the commotion sparkled in the few remaining shafts of light, creating a surreal atmosphere. Danny had the worst of it, meandering around in the dark until Johnson threw her a small handheld torch from his rucksack. She found that she didn't trip over as many things after that. She forced herself not to think about what it was that she was tripping over.

After hearing little on the very creepy journey through the Citadel, there was an almighty cacophony that rose in volume the closer they came to the central spire. There were survivors! The noise gave them hope; hope that someone, somehow was holding out against the Shadows. They doubled their speed as they began to hear evidence of a pitched battle, moving at breakneck pace through doorways and around corners. Such was their haste that they didn't worry about what was waiting for them as they barrelled up the Citadel, concerned only with aiding the survivors.

Danny had only once been this high in the Citadel, shortly after her rushed introduction to Rhiannon. Her memory of the layout was vague yet was good enough to keep the squad moving up. The rooms became smaller and smaller until at last, they burst through a doorway into what was a very out of place waiting room – the room where the Lord Regent made his visitors wait for hours before seeing them, cementing his power over the supplicants further still.

It was gaudily decorated in gold and silvers. This was a room meant to intimidate but it was also a room that showcased how knowledgeable and powerful the Lord Regent was. Arrayed in cases along the walls were Magickal artefacts, some of them glowing or vibrating with the energy that they contained. Danny wished for all the worlds that she could spend some time here, investigating and learning about the heritage of the Order. She was sure that she could learn so much from them that she was almost overcome with excitement. A loud crash brought her back down to Earth (where did these sayings come from?) and she refocused her attention on the plain, unassuming door leading through to the Lord Regent's office.

The rest of the squad did the same, four rifles and a pistol pointing directly at the source of the noise. The door was shut tight but they could hear the battle taking place in the room beyond as if it were happening right next to them. It sounded like two old-world titans had risen from the dead and were having a fistfight, each blow shaking the foundations of the Citadel. Reynolds had been stood next to a battery of artillery in the past and the noise they made was nothing compared to the noise they were now hearing.

"There are survivors through that door," Reynolds said. "They might need our help. We need to think outside the box and come up with alternative solutions. Our rifles may be ineffective so make use of your grenades and flashbangs. We might not be able to kill a Shadow outright but we can do our best to distract it. Baker, I want you to sit this one out. Stay here and guard the door and make sure that nothing comes through after us, got it?"

Baker was not pleased. "But, Sarge, I can still fight! Let me help, please!"

"I'm sorry, Baker. I need you here."

"Yes, Sarge." Baker sighed and went over to the desk that may or may not have been used by a receptionist. He kicked it over and made himself comfortable, dropping his rucksack to the ground and using the lip of the table as a rest for his pistol. "Nothing will get past me, I promise."

"Good lad. Everyone ready?" Reynolds was impressed at how quickly Baker accepted his assignment.

The remaining members of the squad nodded back at him, not trusting their voices to hide their fear. Reynolds squared up to the final door and kicked it once above the lock. With no resistance and minimal noise, the door swung open and the squad charged through, sans Baker.

#

The only person that wasn't surprised was Danny. She had been here once before but even that one visit wasn't enough to stop the size of the office from taking her breath away. It looked vastly different from the last time she was here, but even so, it was still impressive.

On her previous visit, she had seen that the room had been large and domed, with an aperture in the roof for a celestial telescope. There was an oak screen (imported all the way from Earth) around the periphery of the room that would allow a person to walk around the edge without seeing what was happening in the middle. The difference between the room from her memory and the room in its current state was vast and she wasn't sure that she was in the same place. The waiting room that they had just been through was the only thing that convinced her that they were.

The roof was gone. It had been beautifully decorated. Gemstones had been used to lay out the constellations as seen from Earth, rubies, emeralds and sapphires, so large that they must have been priceless, spread out in a stunning vista. Danny felt a moment's anguish when she saw that the roof had been blown away, the Midway night sky hanging where the gems used to be, no less impressive for the lack of jewels. To make matters worse, it was on fire and looked like it was beyond saving.

The oak screen had been blasted away in places, allowing an onlooker a much better view of the centre of the office. All of the furniture that had been here before was either in splinters or burning, the thick smoke only wafting out of the way in intervals. They couldn't see what was going on but they could still hear it, the volume now assailing their eardrums.

Reynolds motioned with his hand, barely visible through the black smoke and his team spread out behind the remains of the oak screen. They filtered carefully around the edge of the room to try and make sense of the situation. They weren't completely successful but they saw enough of the layout that Reynolds could come up with the start of a plan, the view from each member of his team popping up on his HUD.

"Johnson, take Sinclair and climb up to the platform by the telescope," he said over the radio. "Haley, you're with me. We're gonna go left and find a good firing position if one is available. Danny, stay here. If anything comes at you, go back through the door and rendezvous with Baker. He'll look after you and together you might be able to find a way to escape from this nightmare and warn the outside world about what happened here."

With that said and with nothing else to add, they moved off. Danny knelt down behind the remains of a sofa, straining her eyes to catch a glimpse of what was causing the explosions. Try as she might, she couldn't make out anything clearly enough to be sure who was winning or even who was involved in the fight.

One thing she was sure of was that the Lord Regent was in the room and he was engaged in a contest for his own life. It would make sense as she was standing in his office and she knew that he was powerful enough to outlast the rest of the Order. A flash of anger distracted her as she thought that he should have done a better job of looking after those who had died below and the Magick within whispered its agreement. It almost seemed to be saying to her that anyone with that sort of power should have used it to protect, rather than control. Its method of drawing attention from Danny seemed to change in each situation, leaving her ultimately none the wiser of its true intentions, if indeed, it had any.

181

She had lost sight of the squad and wondered where they were, wishing uselessly that she had one of their helmets. Looking left and then right, she tried to spy where they had gone but couldn't see anything worth noting, the size of the room conspiring with the smoke to make her clueless.

A minute dragged by and then another with still no indication that Reynolds had made contact. She didn't know if he was alive and had no way to know if anyone was injured. She daren't drop her mental shield to check for even the shortest time in case the Shadows were able to take control of her mind away from her. She became ever more concerned until she was unable to stop herself from moving, heading in the same direction that she had seen Johnson and Sinclair disappear. It was a good thing that she did.

Not a second after she had moved away from the burning sofa, a large crystal globe came pelting through the smoke and smashed into it, sending shrapnel flying in every direction. She only saw it coming at the last second and a large splinter flew at her head, faster than she had thought possible. She ducked and almost tripped over a fallen ladder but wasn't quick enough to get out of the way completely. The wood made contact with the side of her head and she lost consciousness.

#

How long she had blacked out for, she would never know. When she came round, she could hear gunfire and additional bursts of light told her that the squad were alive and had begun using flashbangs. There was something warm and sticky running down her face and she reached up with her right hand as the other was currently caught underneath her body. She looked at her hand and was surprised to see blood. Was it her blood?

It was. She panicked and tried to stand up, only to fall back to the ground again when a wave of dizziness and the world's worst headache attacked her at the same time. She lay there quietly, struggling unsuccessfully to control her pain. This was the second time today that she had been in this sort of situation and it was becoming very annoying.

Without a choice to the contrary, she looked down at the ground, spotting the single peony that she had taken from Rhiannon's room sitting alone amongst the debris on the floor and looking the worse for wear. Her eyes welled up and she rubbed them with her hand, the stinging only exacerbating the tears that threatened to spill out onto her dusty cheeks.

Minutes passed and the ruckus continued around her. With her headache now firmly under her control, she tried again to stand, first kneeling slowly and allowing herself time to adjust. This time she was successful.

Most of the smoke had cleared out through the roof, propelled on its way by random outbursts of energy which allowed Danny a better view of proceedings. Time slowed for her as she tried to process what her eyes were showing her. She glanced at the edges of the room, catching sight of Johnson and Sinclair both firing over the handrail on the platform. A flashbang grenade was gradually floating towards the middle of the room. The two of them looked like they were in one piece and she felt relief.

The same could not be said of Reynolds and Haley. A look to her left showed her that Haley was down, huge cracks blossoming along the chest piece of her armour, clearly causing her a huge amount of pain. That wasn't the worst bit. Reynolds was knelt at her side, trying desperately to administer first aid as Haley screamed, looking in horror at where her left leg was supposed to be.

They were alive, at least. That was something, more than she could have hoped for, although the longer this continued, the more likely it was that one of the team would die. Now sure that her friends, those wonderful people who had saved her from the jungle, were not in any immediate danger, she turned her attention to the centre of the room – and almost blacked out again.

The Lord Regent was indeed in the room, sweat pouring steadily down his bald head due to the intense concentration and focus he was displaying. He was stood barely a metre away from the largest Shadow that Danny had ever seen.

The Shadow was two metres tall and vaguely humanoid in shape. Its outline was blurry, as if Danny was looking at something that wasn't really there or trying to locate something deep underwater. It was emanating a feeling of pure hatred and the Magick whispered to her gently, helping her to focus and allowing her to pinpoint exactly what its intentions were.

As Danny felt for herself the disdain that the Shadow felt for the Order, she started and caused time to once again come back to normal.

Despite all of the energy being released and the furniture being thrown around the room, the two figures were motionless. The only indication that they were awake was a tornado of metal and wood swirling around them, keeping them penned in like a prison. Danny saw the Lord Regent's eyes flicker to the side and an armchair came rocketing towards the shadow. Suddenly, the armchair decided that it did not, in fact, want to hit the Shadow so it zoomed off in another direction. The Shadow had added energy to its momentum when it redirected the piece of furniture so it collided with the wall and fractured into a thousand pieces.

How could Danny, barely a teenager, help the Lord Regent against something as unstoppable as this? What was she expected to do? Run up to it and give it a kick? That would be absurd. She entertained the thought for a brief moment but decided that she would have to come up with another way to intervene in the battle.

A recent memory came back to her like an old black and white movie playing in her mind. Reynolds was telling the team that they could only hope to distract, not kill. That was something that she could do. The battle was evenly poised and perhaps a small intervention from Danny could tip the scales in favour of the Lord Regent. She would just have to be careful not to distract the Lord Regent himself or it was game over.

She looked around for something to throw at the Shadow, not stopping to think about how she would get it through the torrent of debris. She saw a small rock lying casually on the floor and started in recognition. It was about the size of her closed fist and it was part of the Citadel Rock that she had destroyed during her testing. Perfect!

She grabbed it in both hands, marvelling at how heavy it was before moving it into her right hand. Slowly, she staggered towards the tornado in the middle of the room and threw the hand holding the rock behind her, preparing to throw it. She launched it at her target. Throughout all of this, she hadn't thought once about using her Magick, not yet accustomed to having that particular ace up her sleeve. In all the pandemonium, she had completely drowned out the voice of the Magick and it sat at the back of her mind, sulking sullenly.

Somehow, the rock went through the debris screen and went straight at the Shadow. Danny felt a surge of joy, hoping that the rock would make contact. It nearly did.

Inches from the outline of the Shadow, it stopped. The hope disappeared and then died completely as Danny felt the Shadow turn its attention to her, dismissing the Lord Regent with a burst of energy that sent him flying towards the edge of the room. He hit the oak panelling at high speed and Danny heard a crack.

What was she going to do now? There was nothing she had, no ability or plan that would allow her to defend herself from the Shadow let alone go on the attack. She was frozen like a rabbit in headlights, unable to move away, barely able to breathe. She was shaking so intensely that her teeth were chattering.

As the Shadow mentally reached out to her and physically extended a tendril of itself to grab her, Danny went insane.

29

CHAPTER TWENTY-NINE

It started when she lost her vision. The world went black as the room disappeared from her sight and she cowered, waiting for the Shadow to touch her. What would happen when it did, she didn't know but she was sure that it would be awful, remembering how she had felt in the clearing with the body of her Master. Her thoughts turned instantly to her family and she felt extreme anguish, sorry that she had never had the chance to say a proper goodbye to her loved ones. She spent an eternity in the darkness waiting for a blow that would never come. She tried to protect her body by curling into the foetal position and, remembering one of the last lessons that her Master had imparted to her before her death, she built a wall filled with happy memories of her mum and dad around her young and fragile mind.

After what felt like years, yet, at the same time only seconds, she opened her eyes and started to investigate the area around her, curious about what she would find. The final blow that she had been expecting had never landed and she started to think that there might be a way out of this place. Despite the darkness that had felt so impenetrable, she could just about make out some details and landmarks that hadn't been there at first. It seemed that she was standing in the very room that moments ago (or years) she had been fighting in. There was one major difference, however – this was the Lord Regent's office as it had been, not as it had become.

All the furniture was back in its rightful place, no longer on fire or in pieces. The telescope that had dominated most of the room was restored and looking very shiny as if it had recently been polished by some poor apprentice. Danny raised her head to the ceiling and spent two weeks lost in the sparkle coming from the now perfect gemstones lining the roof. She spotted the Plough and the North Star; she was fascinated with Orion's Belt and she got lost whilst investigating Mars and Jupiter.

It took her an aeon to notice that there was someone sitting at the Lord Regent's desk. She caught movement out of the corner of her eye and swung her gaze to fix on the man lounging in the comfortable-looking chair, his feet up on the desk and his hands clasped behind his head. This was someone she didn't know and she was again afraid.

"You know me, child," the man said and smiled at her. Danny looked again. There was something familiar about this man and his smile but she couldn't quite put her finger on where she knew him from…

With a sudden flash of insight, she recognised him. It was his eyes that did it, coupled with that stupid smile. The Lord Regent's green eyes peered at her over the desk and he lowered his legs and arms. Sitting forward, he cupped his chin in his hands and placed his elbows on the leather top of the desk.

"Yes, you have it correctly. This is how I looked when I was only a young Apprentice, still far from the top of the pyramid but with enough ambition for ten people."

"Where? How? What!" Danny was struggling to get her words out coherently.

"Shall we answer those questions in order? We do have all the time in the world, after all. Or barely any time left, however you choose to look at it." The Lord Regent seemed to be revelling in Danny's confusion, going out of his way to compound it. He motioned to a chair that had appeared on the opposite side of the desk as if by Magick.

Danny hesitated for a fraction of a second but then acquiesced. If this was truly the Lord Regent, she had better do as he said or pay the price.

The seat was incredibly comfortable, at odds with its spindly, wooden appearance. It took all of her effort not to fall asleep after the amount of energy she had expended over the last twelve hours. Or was it twelve years? She wasn't sure.

"Let us start where all good stories commence – the beginning. Not my beginning though, only the start of your inhabitancy in this mind space." Danny started to ask a question but was cut off by the Lord Regent. "Despite appearances, we do not have much leeway. I expect you to keep your silence until I am finished. If we then have time, I will answer any questions you may have. Do you understand?"

Danny nodded. "Yes, Master."

"Good. You would be correct in thinking that this construct in which we find ourselves is not real, at least to those in the outside world. The Shadow, as you keep calling it, is inching ever closer to you whilst we have this chat. We are, in short, in your mind. I used a considerable amount of energy to get here so we must make the most of it. I shall not get another chance and what I have to tell you is of the utmost importance."

More questions occurred to Danny but she did as the Lord Regent bade and kept her peace. It was incredibly difficult to do so as each new question that occurred to her burned brightly in her mind, making them even more obvious to the Lord Regent.

"You are learning. I believe that answers the where, so let us move on to the what. I am losing the battle with the Shadow. I am dying. I possess far too much knowledge to allow it to cease to exist though, so I created this space to impart as much of it to you as I can. Although you would not have been my first choice, you were the only one available so I will make do. You may experience some side effects of the transfer which could be... unpleasant."

A distinct tingling sensation had been building in Danny temples but it wasn't until the Lord Regent mentioned possible side effects that she took notice of it. Now that she was thinking about it, the sensation started to become very uncomfortable.

"The Shadow (silly name, by the by) is an entity belonging to a race of incorporeal beings called the Chosen. The collective races of the Hegemony know very little about them and that is something that I am rather proud of. It was common knowledge once that the races that inhabit the galaxy now were not the first – there was instead a race of beings so advanced that they alone held dominion over the Milky Way. They were the first users of Magick and I believe that despite the obvious advantages of its use, it ultimately became their downfall. The Order has been systematically collecting all traces and remains of this race because we knew that one day, hopefully in the distant future, they would come back to challenge us. It appears that day has come much sooner than we expected. Once again, this is a long story so I would appreciate it were you not to interrupt. I can feel my mind beginning to drift and if you distract me, I fear that I will never be able to tell you the full tale. Are you ready?"

Danny nodded once again, not willing to open her mouth lest the questions began pouring out in an unending rush. The Lord Regent began his story and Danny gasped aloud.

#

When the galaxy was still young, there began a race amongst the emergent species to lay claim to the vast resources scattered amongst the stars. As the Milky Way was still in its infancy, resources were scarcer than they are now and being denied vital minerals or life-giving water could be the death knell of a young society. Competition was fierce, each species in an arms race against the others to lay claim to planet upon planet. At first, it was relatively peaceful – there was room to expand without border clashes or combat. In time, this would change and the change would not be for the better.

There was a species, younger than the others, who blossomed on a planet very similar to Earth. They were inquisitive, producing genius after genius and testing the limits of what a civilisation could achieve. In time, they began to explore, first their solar system and then ranging further afield. They met with other species and formed friendships and rivalries, integrating themselves into the galactic society with an ease that had not been seen before. Despite being able to discover this glut of information, the Order was unable to find a name for this species. I will explain why shortly.

This species, this civilisation of savants, was the first to use Magick. Imagine! With practice, they could manipulate space and time to mould it to their needs, allowing them to progress much faster than their competitors. They soon filled the remaining available space and began to dominate in politics, rising to ever-higher positions of power. It was a true golden age the likes of which has not been seen since.

As with most golden ages, it was too good to last and the downfall would be catastrophic for all.

There was born into this society a youngster who was different from the others. Where they saw peace and cooperation as the pinnacle of society, he looked at what had been created and saw only opportunity. Why should they coexist with races who didn't have the same talents as they, the same natural ability to rise? He was corrupted by Magick and corruption became his trade – and he was incredibly good at it. While he was still young, he rose to the top of the pyramid and began supplanting those who believed in good. He began twisting minds and thoughts, slowly but surely bending others to his will until he was almost in complete control.

It was here the trouble began to spill out into the greater galaxy. Using Magick, he began experimenting with a way to extend his life. In secret, he began abducting the homeless, the sick and the weak and trying to find a way to take their life force to increase his own. It took him years but he was ultimately successful. He would live forever!

The other races found out what he was doing. There was a huge uproar and the galaxy came together in combined anger, casting him down from his perch atop the pile and exiling him to a desolate planet in the outer reaches of the Milky Way. For a time, peace and prosperity returned to the galaxy. It was not to last.

This young Being was convinced that he alone had the right and the power to recreate the galaxy in his own image. Over the course of a decade, he lured travellers and thrill-seekers to his prison and enslaved them, breaking their minds and taking control. As his influence and power grew, so did the hunger. Every use of Magick made him thirst for more and he became a destroyer. When he judged that the time was right, he took his small army to the homeworld of one of the most peaceful races in the galaxy and conquered them without fuss or trouble. When they were completely subjugated, he started teaching his followers how to steal life essences away from others and they began to drain the natives.

After a long and agonising year, the entire population were dry husks, desiccated and lifeless. His followers were stronger than they had ever been and they began to experience the same hunger as this young Being. As strong as they were, the Being was stronger. He alone could give them more; he alone could show them how to satisfy the intense cravings. From this point, his ascendancy was all but assured.

The Milky Way's first crusade began. Planet after planet, civilisation after civilisation fell to the Being and his followers, his ranks and reach swelling with each victory. Governments began to bow down to him, hoping that they would be spared when he came to make his demands of them. They weren't. This Being was so hungry for power that the Milky Way burned with the fires of war until very little was left to oppose him.

Desperately seeking a way to stop him, the remaining members of his species constructed bunkers and laboratories in unlikely places. It was in these desolate and isolated places that they experimented with Magick themselves, looking for a way to either defeat or contain him. This was not natural to them, to use Magick in this way and their proficiency grew incrementally. Centuries and generations passed and their territory dwindled until they were left with a single bastion, a single citadel against the tide. They made their last stand as the enormous war fleet of the immortal Being descended on their planet – on Midway.

Somehow, they stopped the Being. We do not know exactly how they did it but we do know their attempt was successful and we can see the lasting effects of their actions. The Being and his armies were released from their corporeal forms and banished into another realm, a dimension separate from ours where they were imprisoned with no hope of escape. The few weary and relieved survivors of the action vowed never to repeat his mistake and tried to rebuild their society. They failed, unable to retrain themselves towards living a life of peace and growth once more. They had been focused on one goal for so long that they could not remember another way of living. The last vestiges of life in the Milky Way dwindled and disappeared. Until we evolved.

We found ruins and tombs spread across countless planets. The first investigators believed that there was a race of gods who had come before then, calling them the Chosen. When they discovered that they were ruled by one person, they took to calling him the Chosen King. It is this Being that we now fight against in the Citadel. How ironic that the last place he fought when he was alive is now the first place he is fighting when he is all but dead.

They come for you, child. You embody within you such power, power of a like that has not been seen in the galaxy since the days of the Chosen King. He wants to steal it from you, hoping that you would be the final piece in the puzzle that would allow him to bring his full force to bear on the Milky Way once more. If he succeeds, everyone and everything you know will bow down to him within a matter of years.

We brought you here to protect you. We have failed. It is now your turn to protect us. If you cannot weather the storm, the Chosen King will return and we will all be doomed.

30

CHAPTER THIRTY

Danny had been sitting deadly still, enthralled by the tale that was being spun for her. As the Lord Regent completed recounting the history of the Shadows – of the Chosen – Danny felt an odd sense of relief underlined with intense terror. *No pressure,* she thought, *just the fate of all living being in my hands. The hands of a thirteen-year-old!*

"What's supposed to happen now?" Danny asked, desperately hoping that the Lord Regent would provide her with an answer or a way out of her supposed fate. He didn't disappoint her, not entirely.

"I am unable to help any more than I already have, child. What happens next is up to you. I have given you my knowledge and my power, keeping only enough to finish this conversation. It is no small thing that I have done so I expect to be remembered and honoured beyond measure. A statue in the courtyard would be the minimum, wouldn't you agree?" He smiled. That damned smile.

Danny smiled back.

"I think I know what to do," she said, feeling a confidence that she hadn't expected. "I know what to do but not how. Help me, please!"

"Trust your instincts. Sometimes, on those rare occasions when your own intelligence or strength fails you, the Magick only needs pointing in the right direction."

"You speak of Magick as if it has a mind of its own. How can this be?"

"A question for another time, I think. One that you will have to find an answer for on your own." The Lord Regent seemed paler than he had when he had started his tale. As Danny watched, he continued to fade until she could see through him to the wall behind. She thought that this meant he was dying. She didn't want to say that out loud but she didn't need to. She'd forgotten that the Lord Regent was not only incredibly adept at reading thoughts but was also present in her mind.

"Yes, I am dying. I have done what I needed to and now I go on my next adventure." His calmness was at odds with the torrent of emotions that Danny was feeling. How could he be so relaxed, knowing that he was dying?

"I know what awaits on the other side. You will find out yourself one day. Unless… A final warning. What the Chosen King will have to offer you will be tempting, more so than anything else you have ever been given. Do not follow him down his path. A fate worse than death awaits anyone who does the bidding of the monstrosity. You must be the flame that lights the way for the rest of the Order. Gather any survivors and prepare, for the Chosen King is only accompanied by a small escort – what is to come is far worse. You will need to unite the galaxy, no small task even for someone many years your elder. It all lies on your shoulders. Trust the soldiers you came here with – through the hardships to come, they may prove to be your greatest allies."

His final words echoed around the dark space, the reverberations getting quieter with each repetition. Danny blinked and the Lord Regent was gone, adventuring where all would one day follow.

#

Left alone in the recesses of her own mind, Danny was expecting a flash or a bang, something to indicate that she had snapped back to the real world. Anything would have done, really. Nothing happened. She was still sitting at the desk but was now on the other side without having been aware that she had moved. Her perspective had changed and she realised that she was now sitting in the Lord Regent's chair. How had that happened? She didn't know.

The tingling in her temples had grown until it encompassed her entire body. She stood, scraping the chair back on the floor and tipping it over, causing a loud crash that made her jump. It was uncomfortable and was growing ever more painful by the second (month?).

She sauntered around the office, trying to look for a way out of the space in her mind. There was nothing obvious, nothing that jumped out at her and said, 'This way!' Danny became more and more frustrated so distracted herself by looking around the room, searching for her friends.

The scene had changed whilst she had been talking to the Lord Regent; each person had moved ever so slightly from where they had been when she first arrived here. The shadow – the Chosen King, she had to remind herself – had halved the distance to her, its arm reaching towards her and rising higher with each passing second. She walked up to him and had a good look, hoping for a glimpse of the person underneath the blurry outline. She was disappointed not to see anything and wondered if she would ever see what the race of beings that he had once belonged would once have looked like. She thought that she could sense an awareness under the outline, an old and aged consciousness that held an edge of malice. Not wanting to spend too much time this close to the Chosen King nor delve too deeply into his depths, she turned and searched the room for Reynolds.

She found him mid-shout, still desperately trying to stem the blood flowing quickly from Haley's leg. She checked him over to make sure that he wasn't injured himself and then thought to herself, *I wonder if I can help Haley with my Magick from where I am?*

She reached into that now completely familiar place in her head where the Magick lived and found with a start that the Magick had been waiting to gain her attention. Like speaking to a long-lost friend, she made the connection and felt the power surge through her, directing it along the path she wanted it to take. For the first time, they worked in harmony.

With the room and persons within still moving in slow motion, Danny grabbed Haley's amputated leg and moved it back to where it belonged, not looking too closely at the gory artefact. After lining it up, she blew gently over the wound, watching in amazement as it knitted itself back together until it looked almost as good as new. A small red line was the only thing that remained on the leg, testament to the fact that it had actually been separated from the soldier's body.

Next, she walked across to Sinclair and Johnson. They were still in one piece, the flashbang that she had noticed before making her way across the room still gently floating through the air. The final thing she saw on her route around the room was the single peony that had belonged to Rhiannon, still sat sadly amidst the debris. She walked over and gingerly picked it up, cradling it in her clasped hands. She closed her eyes and willed the flower to come back to life. Feeling a small amount of energy seep out of her, she directed it into the peony and opened her eyes to see a refreshed flower, which she happily slid back into her hair just above her ear.

Satisfied that she had done something to help, she went and sat back in the Lord Regent's chair. Why was she still here? She couldn't think of an answer.

Years passed; Danny didn't move, the scene in front of her inching ever closer to the conclusion.

After a decade, Danny got angry. After a century, she was furious. By the time a millennium had passed, she was ready to explode. She opened her mouth in a wordless scream, allowing all her anger and frustration to flow through her and escape into the ether. For the final time that day, Danny passed out.

31

CHAPTER THIRTY-ONE

"Haley, you're gonna be okay!" Reynolds roared as he scrambled around to find an instrument with which to cauterise the wound on her leg. "You're gonna be fine, just hold on!"

He threw his gaze around the floor desperately. *Please, let me find something that I can help Haley with.* His gaze settled on his rifle which he had thrown away in his mad dash to Haley's side, now ever so slightly out of reach. He would have to let go of Haley to get the rifle but it could save her life – it had an energy release mode that would burn her flesh and stop her from bleeding out. It would hurt like hell but it should do the trick, if only temporarily. The only problem was, to get it, he would have to let her bleed. It was a chance that he would have to take.

His sights still firmly on the rifle and with shrapnel flying over his head to make craters in the soft wooden wall behind him, he was taken unawares when a flashbang went off in the vicinity of the Shadow. He lost his sight and heard nothing but a ringing in his ears. Disoriented, he let go of Haley and staggered away, reaching with his hands to find a stable surface to steady himself. One step, then two and his hands connected with the oak screen set around the room. He shook his head from left to right and tried to clear his vision unsuccessfully. Over an agonising minute, he gradually began to make out faint shapes. He blinked furiously, begging whatever gods there were to help him, to help his squad before something happened that they couldn't reverse. Wherever they were, whoever they were, they listened.

Reynolds regained his vision. He was positioned facing through the oak screen into the middle of the room and quickly identified what was going on. Danny was down. The Lord Regent had collapsed against the far wall, looking for all the world like a puppet with his strings cut, both boneless and lifeless. Johnson and Sinclair were still firing over the banister at the Shadow which was making directly for Danny. He swivelled and saw that Haley had stopped screaming; she was looking in disbelief at her leg – which had Magickally reattached itself! Not believing what his eyes were showing him, he took a step back towards Haley.

"Sarge, I'm fine! Go help Danny!" Haley was just as shocked as he was by this turn of events but her good nature nevertheless came to the fore, demanding that her Sergeant look after the little girl that they had all taken under their collective wings. Reynolds did as he was told.

He turned and ran into the middle of the room with no regard for his own safety. The Shadow was now directly between him and Danny, the young girl who was slumped on the floor. He noted that there was a faint glow surrounding the girl but didn't have time to figure out what that meant. He filed it away in the back of his mind to investigate later and sprinted towards the Shadow.

As he came closer to the Shadow, he saw that it was reaching for Danny, its outstretched hand clenched into an awful claw. Slowly but gracefully, it was raising an arm and reaching for her head, looking bizarrely as if it were reaching out to caress her face. What could he do to stop it?

Guns hadn't been effective and flashbangs had only distracted it for a short time. The only reason they had survived this long was because the Shadow had been locked in battle with the Lord Regent, only the barest amount of its attention directed towards the soldiers who were buzzing around like flies on the periphery. There was nothing left in his arsenal which could possibly help – yet, if he did nothing, Danny would surely be killed by this demon.

Acting on instinct, he dove towards the creature, hoping that he could make contact with it and move it away from Danny long enough that she could regain consciousness and escape. He flew through the air, wondering if this was the time and place of his death.

The Shadow wasn't there. Rather, it looked as if it were there but Reynolds blew through it as if it were made of smoke. His reactions were good enough that when he came out the other side, he converted the forwards dive into a roll and came to a stop just in front of Danny. Crouching right in front of her, he had a moment of clarity as he accepted that he would have to sacrifice himself for the young girl.

The world seemed to stop as he looked at her young face. She was clearly still unconscious but looked peaceful and untroubled, as if she were only sleeping. A feeling of intense pride and protectiveness washed over him and he wondered if any children he may have in the future would be anything like Danny. It seemed unlikely because he was sure that this would be where he died – he was willing to give his life if it meant even one of his friends and colleagues escaping from the hell-hole this planet had become.

These feelings came and went in but a second before a feeling of calm descended on him. He took one last, agonisingly long look at Danny's face and then stood up to his full height and turned to face the Shadow.

"I won't let you have her," he said, wondering if the Shadow could understand him. "I'll die before I let you touch her."

The Shadow faltered and Reynolds thought that it was unsure about what he intended. Against all hope, he thought that Danny might escape.

"Johnson," he whispered from the corner of his mouth, "come and pick her up. Get her out of here!"

He wasn't sure if Johnson had got the message as there was no movement behind him. He tried again, repeating the message over and over whilst the Shadow stayed rooted to the spot, swaying backwards and forwards as if waiting for something.

A faint scuffling eventually sounded from behind him and before he could react, the Shadow sprung forward as if released from a spell. Reynolds closed his eyes, the only thing he could do before he knew the Shadow would dispose of him, wondering if he would be aware of his surroundings when he had the black ooze seeping out of his eyes and down his bare skin. Would he be aware, trapped in his body and mind? Or would it be like passing away, blissfully unaware of what was happening to his physical remains?

A hand landed on his shoulder and his eyes snapped open just in time to see the Shadow go flying across the room as if possessed. Was it running? He couldn't tell but it didn't seem like something that the Shadow would do. Pushing it from his mind for a second, he turned around to see who had put their hand on his shoulder.

Standing placidly in front of him was a young woman, perhaps in her early twenties. This was someone new, he realised. She was blonde with an elfin face and features that he vaguely recognised. Glancing down, he saw that the woman was wearing the blue robes of an apprentice of the Order, although they looked very small on her. He was sure he had never seen this woman before and it wasn't until he noticed the single peony tucked gently and with care behind the woman's ear that he made the connection.

"Danny?"

32

CHAPTER THIRTY-TWO

Danny didn't know why Reynolds was looking at her so strangely, nor did she know why she felt so light and full of energy. She did know that she was going to make the most of it and her initial push towards the Chosen King had resulted in the Being catapulting away from her much faster than she had intended. She moved her hand away from Reynolds' shoulder and put it on his cheek, all her love and admiration for him manifesting itself in this simple action.

"Take the others and leave," she said. Reynolds stared at her and then nodded, stepping around her and heading for the exit with Danny watching him the whole way. As he went, he ordered Johnson and Sinclair to get Haley and waited for them at the door, holding it open in a show of chivalry out of place in the war-torn room. The door closed gently behind him and Danny turned to face the Chosen King, a look of determination on her face.

"You know who I am and I know who you are," she said and took a step forward. The Chosen King mirrored her movement with only the barest hesitation, both now slowly walking towards each other in a bizarre facsimile of an old western shoot-out.

"You've killed the Lord Regent so I assume you think you have the upper hand. Unluckily for you, you failed to stop him from helping me and he prepared me for this moment. I know what will happen if I allow you to win. You'll sweep through the galaxy, completing the mission you set out on millennia ago. This I will not allow."

Danny was shocked at how calm and authoritative her voice sounded but took it in her stride, attributing the change to the huge flow of Magick crackling at her fingertips. The build-up of energy was so great that as she raised her hand in front of her face in wonder, a small fork of lightning shot off towards the edge of the room. She smiled. She lowered her hand and looked back at the Chosen King, feeling the static sizzling around her body.

Getting closer to each other, they began to reach out with their minds and use their Magick to try to penetrate the other's defence. Danny was prepared for this, preparing a shield so strong around her thoughts that the Chosen King had no opportunity to slip through.

This shield was not just made from the memories of her family – this shield included memories of Rhiannon, the Lord Regent, of Reynolds, Johnson, Baker, Haley and Sinclair. This shield was created and maintained by all the people who had ever loved her, who had ever supported her and who had prepared her for this moment.

She went on the attack. Using the Magick in ways that she shouldn't have known, she grabbed the outline of the Chosen King and began to pull. The mental probes attacking her shield lessened as the Chosen King redirected the energy to protecting his outline and Danny took another step forward. Backwards and forwards went the battle for control and, for a while, it seemed as if they were evenly matched. Another bolt of lightning left Danny and shot towards the Chosen King, distracting him for the split second that Danny required to take command. She smiled once more, this time in victory, and then found herself scrabbling for purchase on the floor as the Chosen King took another approach in a desperate attempt to fight back. As one, they began rising elegantly into the air, supported no longer by the floor or any earthly thing.

Up they went, beginning to rotate around each other as a raging torrent of debris was swept up and collected in the mental storm. They rose through the roof, out into the cool night air and away from the Citadel, higher and higher into the atmosphere. Still mentally attacking each other, their meteoric rise through the air came to a halt two miles above the surface and Danny could see the awe-inspiring vista of Midway in every direction.

Her mental purchase on the Chosen King became stronger again as she used the memories of the last twenty-four hours to fuel her anger rather than her shield. She could see where she had landed in the Lukratza's base with Master Rhiannon. She could see where her Master had died and where she had met Geoff Reynolds and his team of amazing, empathetic and supremely talented people. She could see where the royal assault force had made their last stand (how did she know about that?) and she could see where the Lukratza commander had met his makers.

She started, almost falling through the air as she realised that these last few thoughts were not her own. They were the memories of the Chosen King – there was no way she could possibly know about them otherwise. Her attacks were working!

She doubled down on her assault, using her experiences and her feelings to attack the Chosen King in a way he wouldn't know how to counter. She was human and humans were known for being emotional. The Chosen King wasn't. He simply couldn't handle the feelings that Danny was forcing on him, having spent so long trapped in a prison of his own making. Even before he was imprisoned, he was merciless and would commit crimes that no sane person would ever dream of doing. To him, feelings just did not compute.

She was close to a breakthrough; she could feel that if she could only summon a bit more strength, she might escape this mess. If she couldn't push through now, there was no second chance. Despite having had a small insight into the mind of the Chosen King, she was no closer to understanding him.

She was going to fail. She wasn't strong enough to win this fight and that meant she was going to let her friends down. Reynolds and the guys would be killed and it would be all her fault! She felt despair. It wasn't fair!

The strength of her emotions gave her a surge of energy. The Magick almost seemed to say to her, *it isn't your fault. Together, we can do this. Push!*

So, she pushed, through the inky black barriers that the Chosen King had thrown up to protect himself and deep into the murky depths of his soul. Caught unawares by the scale of her success, Danny succumbed to a stream of memories that were flowing in the opposite direction, struggling to keep them in some sort of order.

#

He was lonely as a youngling, always being shunned by his peers as they saw that he was different. He was once hit in the head by a rock and laughed at by the others as they stood around him in a circle calling him names.

He was especially adept at using Magick. He had been a natural, intuitively playing with small items and making them fly around, often making his mother smile at him with pride. It wasn't until he was much older that he realised what it could truly be used for.

He remembered the first time he had been elected to office, proud of his achievements and those of his race. He had stood at the front of a large crowd, the chanting and cheering very different from his peers taunting but giving him an inner warmth that he had never felt before.

He knew that he could change things for the better. He knew that he could use his innate powers to improve the situation of his species, if only they stopped being so stubborn and resistant to new ideas. He was right, gods damn them, and those morons should listen to him!

The shame when he was cast from society was strong. It wasn't personal shame – he still believed that he was right and they were wrong. He was instead ashamed that his kind were unable to understand him and had doomed themselves to failure, to mediocrity. He would show them; he swore it when they left him on that forsaken planet.

The look on the beast's face when he transferred its life essence into him was sincerely satisfying. He had caught them in his trap, giving them a small taste of what they could achieve if they only listened to him. His plans to escape the planet were beginning to bear fruit and he knew that it was now only a matter of time.

Years and billions of miles later, he was nearly there. He had spent so long getting to this point, he was sure that he couldn't fail. He had millions of soldiers, hundreds of thousands of battleships and only had to take control of the last enclave of his people. It was so close that he could taste it – the adulation and the years upon unending years of control, of shaping the galaxy to be a haven for all peoples. The only thing worrying him was the hunger. Would it ever go away?

He remembered waking up in the darkness with no idea how he had gotten there. He remembered screaming and shouting in pain as the energy he had relied on his entire life was no longer there. His followers looked at him in dismay as they realised they were trapped. Where could they go? What could they do? Nothing, it seemed. For thousands of years, nothing.

Until… Until they felt something come to life. Something that would be their salvation. They once again tasted Magick, using the dregs that filtered through to them to construct another fleet, much smaller and less impressive than the one he had commanded at the pinnacle of his power. The Chosen King was still strong and sucked down as much of the power as he could, until at long last, he pierced through the veil separating the wasteland that they inhabited and the Milky Way. They boiled through, not all of his army, not yet – just enough to help him capture the key to their escape.

A man called James had been his first victim in years. They had sucked the human ship dry, learning as they went about the new species, the new government which still clearly oppressed all forward thinkers.

They had seen Danny in a video and knew right away that she was the one.

Light years of space had been crossed at speed. They had arrived at the planet Midway, which the Chosen King realised was the planet where the last of his species had made their stand. Carving through the human fleet with ease, they had made planetfall and had begun the hunt. What a glorious hunt it had been. What an ignominious end.

The girl had been stronger than the Chosen King had ever imagined. He didn't understand the feelings that she was forcing onto him, had never dreamed of feeling such things again. It was to be his undoing. It was too much!

#

Danny understood. She felt his pain, his humiliation and accepted it as her own. She had now lived through his entire life and understood that what he was, was not what he had hoped to become. He could not be killed, only diverted. There was only one thing that would defeat him and Danny knew what it was.

Danny forgave him. She told him that it wasn't his fault, that he was a slave to the Magick. She told him that he would never have done these things if only he'd had the choice. It was the others, they made him do it. Danny absolved him of his sins and he hated her for it. He left.

The tenuous grasp the Chosen and their King had held on this reality disappeared and they were banished back to their own realm. Midway was silent for the first time since the beginning of the Dùbhlan. The victors and the vanquished were both few in numbers but they were no longer in danger because Danny, the thirteen-year-old in the body of a twenty-something, had conquered not only her own fears but the fears of the Chosen King.

Danny cheered, her voice dissipating in the wind at this great height and then realised there was one problem left to solve, at least for today. How in the worlds was she going to get down from here?

33

Chapter Thirty-Three

It's amazing, Danny thought, *the difference a day makes*. She had eventually lowered herself back down to the Citadel, landing gently (and with a little embarrassment) back in the Lord Regent's office in front of a very happy but inquisitive Reynolds.

With the departure of the Chosen, communications in the Midway system had been fully restored and Reynolds wasted no time in summoning help, both from the Empire and from the Hegemony. Support ships raced to the planet, bringing troops and supplies to help the survivors. Behind them came the news reporters, eager to find out what had caused such a strange situation. They were forbidden from broadcasting their findings pending the results of the Hegemony's official investigation but Danny thought this was a mistake. The Chosen were going to come back; she knew it, and the citizens of the galaxy would be better off if they knew they had to prepare for something.

The Magick that she embodied was so powerful that it couldn't help but seep across the void, allowing the Chosen another opportunity to break free. They had to be prepared, had to work together if they were to stand a chance against them and Danny was convinced that withholding information from the general population wasn't the way to do that.

To her surprise, the few survivors of the Order had gathered around her in admiration when she descended through the Citadel. They had felt the strength of the clash of energies at the summit of the tower and more than one of them had received a quick mental visit from the Lord Regent before his death. He had explained to the few remaining Masters what had happened and they now deferred to Danny, with more than one offering her the title of Lord Regent. She had declined, at least for now, not wishing to be caught in the petty bureaucracy of the Order's internal politics.

Danny herself was struggling to come to terms with the changes that she had undergone. She was no longer thirteen, of that, she was sure. Physically, she had the body of a woman ten years older and one of the Masters suggested that this had been a boon from the Lord Regent to allow her to contain and control the knowledge and power he had given her. She wasn't sure how she felt about that, whether to be thankful or upset that her body had been changed without her permission. What she was sure of was that she wouldn't have been able to defeat the Chosen King without the change, so perhaps acceptance would be the key to her happiness surrounding this issue.

Sergeant Reynolds and his squad had all survived. Baker was currently on a human medical ship in orbit, being fitted for a fancy prosthetic. He was adamant that he wanted it to be decorated with flames and, for some strange reason, an image of a donkey.

Haley was essentially in one piece, her leg requiring no further treatment. She, along with Johnson and Sinclair, had been keeping a watchful eye over Danny since the departure of the Chosen King. A girl left alone in a strange new world, they figured that she could use all the friends she could get.

Colonel Brydges had survived, although only just. He had been playing hide and seek with one of the Chosen moments before they were banished back to their own realm and was profuse in thanking Danny for saving him and his men. He swore there and then that if she were to ever need help, she need only call and they would answer. He never got to use the tanks he had been sent at the start of the Dùbhlan.

Admiral Leystrom and General Webb were back in orbit over Midway, the H.M.S *Excellence* being one of the first to respond to the distress calls coming from the planet. It served as the main point of coordination for the relief efforts with any human survivors brought up to the ship. They also received their first-ever alien visitors, the few Lukratza survivors making a short visit onboard whilst waiting for their own ships to arrive – their fleet has been completely destroyed at some point over the day. Although they refused to give their names to the officer on deck, they were nothing if not polite and complimentary about Reynolds and his squad, whom they had somehow heard of despite the media blackout.

H.M.S. *Excellence* would be the scene of the final gathering over Midway before it departed on its journey back to Earth. When the King had heard about what had happened on Midway, he had immediately recalled the battleship to protect the capital. From what Danny had heard, the vast majority of species were doing the same. Taking the final message of the Lord Regent on board, she had called the meeting between as many species as possible on the human flagship to try and change their minds. It was going to be hard.

The meeting was quick. Despite the clear threat to the combined races of the galaxy, none of them was willing to take the word of the survivors about what had happened on Midway. Disappointed at their response, Danny and Reynolds watched from the flight deck as the various representatives went on their separate ways, intent on ignoring the problem in front of them.

Before leaving H.M.S. *Excellence*, Danny was called into a meeting with General Webb.

#

"What you did down there was nothing short of miraculous," Webb said as he leaned back in his chair, holding a cup of coffee in his hands.

"What I did was necessary," Danny replied. She looked down at her hands, twiddling her thumbs in distraction. "I wouldn't have been able to do it without Sergeant Reynolds, though."

"Geoff speaks very highly of you, young lady." Webb had a small smile. "In fact, I think he wants to adopt you into his squad. It's not going to happen but he was very insistent. He actually started swearing at me."

"I hope you weren't too harsh on him, sir."

"No, I wasn't. What that man has been through – what you all have been through – would have made anyone swear."

"Mmm." Danny wasn't sure how to respond to that. She felt her thoughts wandering, thinking about the Chosen. She hadn't been successful at persuading the other races of the coming threat, but the humans had been very supportive. It had helped that Brydges and Reynolds had survived the conflict, two well-respected soldiers who could be taken at their word.

"What are you thinking about?" Webb asked.

"The Chosen. How can the other races be so blind? We know they're coming and we know how dangerous they are. The only race that sounded even slightly supportive was the Lukratza and they scare me."

"Scare you? You could skin any one of them with but a thought and they scare you?"

Danny flinched when Webb said that. She had the power but she wasn't the sort of person to think of committing such a heinous crime without understanding how wrong it was.

"I would never…" she started before Webb cut her off.

"I know. It was only a comment, made without thought. Accept the apologies of an old man. What are you going to do now?"

"I'm going to try and rebuild the Order. Someone has to be ready for the return of the Chosen. I'm going to scour all records in the archive and learn as much as I can, both about the Chosen and about Magick."

"Sensible. I wish you luck."

"Thank you, sir. Can I ask what your next move is?"

"You can. I have been recalled to the palace on Earth. I suspect I will have to justify to the King how I managed to lose almost sixty thousand men, despite not actually being in command of them. I'll also have to persuade him of the threat the Chosen pose. He won't have believed any of the reports so it may be a tough proposition."

"Good luck then, sir."

"Good luck to you, Danny. Oh, one last thing before you go. A couple of friends of yours have asked to be assigned as your protection. It's taken some hard work, getting this through the bureaucracy, but you will be pleased to learn that Sergeant Reynolds and the Flaming Donkeys have been temporarily garrisoned at the Citadel. Pending your approval, of course."

Danny was taken aback by the generosity, both of the General and of Reynolds and his squad. "Thank you, sir!"

"Don't thank me yet. You'll find them waiting outside the office, wanting to escort you home. You'll also have to tell me the story about why they are called the Flaming Donkeys some time…"

#

Danny was incredibly pleased to be escorted to the shuttle bay by Reynolds and even happier that they were all coming with her. They didn't say much to each other on the journey down to Midway, only starting to talk when the shuttle was entering the atmosphere.

Danny looked through the hatch at the back of the ship and saw H.M.S *Excellence* hanging majestically, illuminated by the light from the Midway sun. She knew that it was charging its jump drives ready to leave for Earth and felt sad that some of the only remaining humans in the system would soon be leaving.

"Don't worry about them, Danny," Reynolds said when he saw that she was looking worried. "I've had a word with Colonel Brydges and he's gonna do some grafting when he gets back to Earth, drum up as much

211

support for the cause as he can. He knows that you're the only reason he's alive. He'll support you."

"Thank you." Danny was genuinely touched. "Do you think he'll be able to make a difference?"

"I do." Reynolds was quiet for a second. "It's going to be bad, isn't it?"

Danny nodded. "It is. Together, though, we can make sure that we have the best chance possible. If you're willing, there are a couple of places that I would like you guys to go - see what you can find. Not right now, but in the near future."

"Of course."

Those two simple words filled Danny with confidence and it was a feeling that lasted for a long time after the *Excellence* had jumped for Earth, the light from its engines flashing once and signalling that the galaxy had changed forever.

Printed in Great Britain
by Amazon